Journey to
CHESHIRE BAY

USA TODAY BESTSELLING AUTHOR

H.M. SHANDER

AUTHOR'S NOTE

At its heart, this story is about love, hope, and finding yourself.
However, the journey there is often bumpy, unclear, and at many
times, trying.
This book deals with depression and loneliness, and there are
discussions about suicide. I've tried to be sensitive and delicate,
but I understand these words could reopen past scars.
I trust you to know your limits, but to also remind you, you are
never alone.

Suicide Hotline
(Canada) 1.833.456.4566
(USA) 1.800.273.8255

Table of Contents

Chapter One

uicide wasn't the answer, and hindsight was always 20/20.

I knew this to be the truth, but in the present moment, giving a giant fuck-you to the people I thought were my friends and running away made me feel better. Made me feel like I had control.

Naturally, it was all an illusion.

I had control over nothing.

No one cared what I did with my life, where I went, or how I destroyed everything in my wake. My future, if I wanted a fresh start, beckoned me with the promise of something new. All I had to do was survive the flight there. It was now or never.

A voice crackled over the loudspeaker. "Final boarding call for Air Canada flight 127, bound for Vancouver."

Fuck it.

There was no time like the present.

"Just wait," I yelled to no one, as I pushed through a thick crowd of people.

This new urge to take the reins and live the life I wanted – or at least try to – consumed me, propelling me down the lengthy corridors to the gate at the end. There was no way I was missing this flight. Too much was on the line if I had to watch the plane pull away and deal with everything I'd left in the aftermath of my disastrous failure of a life.

I increased my speed and threw my arm through the other strap of my backpack, pulling tight to stop it from slamming against my back with each bouncy step.

I ran double time, rudely yet apologetically pushing the people I was unable to avoid out of my way and screeched to a halt in front of the desired gate.

"Wait, please." Breathlessly, I waved my boarding pass to the flight attendant at the desk.

"I need to see ID." She clicked on the computer without a glance.

Beyond the window, the plane sat still attached to the jetway, the spotlight on her nose highlighting the blanket of darkness surrounding it. Thank goodness it hadn't left yet. The potential for a brand new start still lay ahead.

I rooted through the Coach knockoff I discovered in the bottom of a bargain bin at Goodwill, and pulled out my temporarily invalid driver's license, presenting it with my boarding pass. As I struggled to catch my breath, I swiped my forehead with the back of my hand.

"Seat 34A." She handed back my effects. "Have a safe flight, Iris."

Cringing at the sound of my birth name, since I'd long used a nickname, I slouched as I struggled to regulate my breathing while I walked down the jetway. Damn, I was truly out of shape. The crisp August midnight air mixed with a touch of something unfamiliar; the scent of it getting stronger upon approach.

My legs suddenly froze at the sight of the heavy metal door resting off to the side of the mighty jet, ready to seal my fate. Once that door closed, there was no turning back.

My new beginning was just a mere five feet ahead.

Could I really do it?

All I had to do was step on the plane.

Whether to appease the building ache or to remind myself I wasn't important and had never been, I glanced over my shoulder to the stretched emptiness behind me for one more final check. No one aside from the flight attendant who'd just scanned my boarding pass was in view. Not a 'friend' not a 'family member'.

"Come on in, we're just getting ready for departure." Another airline worker, with a nametag bearing Wendy, waved in a rush.

My hand shook as I held out the boarding pass, but

thankfully, the length of the sleeve kept my tiger stripes from view, although she did stare at my hand longer than I thought was necessary.

"You just made it," she said with a smile as her hand touched my shoulder. Her head bobbed as she attempted to read the shaking seat assignment, until she grabbed the paper firmly. "You're at the back, on the right. Window seat."

A cold sweat washed over me as I left the unsteady jetway and put my foot onto the sturdy floor of the interior of the plane. Passing through the high-priced business class, the passengers glared while I shuffled by their seats, as if I were keeping them from their destinations. But I hadn't. I'd arrived just on time. *Just.* The flight wasn't scheduled to depart for another three minutes.

I stepped beyond the elite seats, into economy where the seats were crammed together, but where most of the passengers sent less than a cursory glance in my direction. Despite the late hour departure, the flight was nearly packed.

The sign above the first section of tightly packed seats indicated row 14. Clearly, at row 34, I was at the far back of the plane, and I shifted my backpack as I inched, reminding myself to breath as I moved towards my escape.

The seconds to change my mind were ticking loudly.

Another flight attendant advanced up the aisle. "Seat?"

"34A." My voice was as jittery as my legs were weak.

This was going to be a long six-hour flight across the

country to my first stop in Vancouver. After a small layover and another short flight, I'd land in Victoria to spend a few hours until my cousin's friend would arrive and fly me over to Cheshire Bay.

My new residence. No more living in my car.

My cousin Amber offered me temporary shelter and solace. It was the break I needed to start fresh.

The flight attendant walked backwards and pointed to the vacant window seat.

Just my luck, I was sharing the space with a guy about my age, and a decently cute one to boot.

"You can store your bags overtop, or under the seat in front of you." The flight attendant pointed to both areas.

"In front of me is better."

My seat mate twisted his legs off into the aisle, allowing me to squeeze into the tiny space I'd paid big bucks for. Dropping into my seat, I didn't miss his cocked eyebrow, followed by a narrowed gaze as he tipped his head questioningly to the side.

What was his problem?

Avoiding eye contact, I tore my focus inward and begged my heartrate and breathing to slow down to acceptable levels. My heart pounded incessantly, not from the running, but from the rapidly fraying thread I believed was my future.

Suddenly, I wasn't so sure I wanted the unknown. Even though things were a disaster, everything here was familiar.

The places, the day to day, the heartache of epic loneliness.

The growing ache switched from a dull pang to weak painful stabs, focused solely on my heart. Was this the end? Was this how I was going to die? From soul-crunching loneliness? At least my original plan gave me a false sense of control over when and how. But this?

It was too much, and I unbuckled, ready to get off. "I'm sorry, I need to go."

The plane rocked, and I threw my gaze out the window to see what the hell was going on. We were leaving; the plane was moving backwards. It seemed the now portion of *now or never* had arrived. No turning back.

"Fuck my life." I whispered as the tears welled up and blurred my view.

My head knocked against the head rest, shifting my messy bun, and I closed my eyes, unable to stop the wave of forthcoming tears.

Voices spoke overhead, pointing out exits and floatation devices, most of which I didn't understand. All I truly heard was *cabin crew doors flight position and cross-check, please.*

That's it, the doors were sealed, and my breath hitched for all that it meant.

"Hey, miss?"

I wiped a damp eye with the edge of my ragged sweatshirt leaving a streak of black from the mascara on the cuff, and I turned to the cute guy, not giving a rat's ass if he saw me in a cringe-worthy condition. I didn't know him, and I most certainly wasn't here for his entertainment. "Yeah?"

"Everything okay?"

"Just frickin' peachy." The words rolled out lacking confidence but ripe with sarcasm.

Truth of the matter - I was a total mess. My stomach was in knots, and I felt like I was having an out of body experience, hovering and staring at myself from above.

"You look so familiar." He tapped his chin. "Do I know you from somewhere?"

"Unless you were a regular at Del's on 86, I'm afraid you're mistaking me for someone else." I ran my gaze slowly down and up him, not letting a morsel of recognition light up my face when it dawned on me who he was.

Truth was an evil bitch.

Whereas he'd changed and morphed from an awkward caterpillar into a handsome butterfly, to the point I barely recognized him, it was the crater above his right eye that gave away his identity. I knew exactly who I was sitting beside.

FML.

Karma wasn't even close to being finished with me yet.

Chapter Two

This was going to be a much longer flight than scheduled. Not only was I terrified about my first ride in a plane as a grown ass adult, now I had to sit next to the nerdy guy I'd picked on in high school for the next six hours as we flew across the country.

Fate or destiny or whatever you want to call it was laughing her fucking ass off. What an unfortunate seat assignment.

I glanced around the cabin, trying to see if there were other vacant seats. All I saw were heads, lots of heads, and no spaces between them.

"You look nervous. Have you ever flown before?"

"Once." When I was three and being flown to my new family. I didn't dare look him in the eyes.

"You know, my sister gets like this when she travels and let me tell you, the first time she flew, well, she was paler than you. Actually, she was a touch green." Hearing his inflections had a weird effect – they actually started to calm me. "What helped her was the vomit bag and some fresh air."

"Are you going to crack a window?"

He chuckled. "You're funny, but no."

A green sweater filled my view, and a second later a blast of cool air was directed at my face. I slammed my eyes shut again as the tentacles of air wrapped their fingers around my neck. Surprisingly enough, it had the opposite intended effect of calmness, and I reached overhead to twist the air off.

"No, thank you."

"Thought I'd offer." He shrugged, a hint of either a New York or Bostonian accent in his voice. "If there's anything I can do to help, let me know."

"Feel free to keep talking; your voice is easy to listen to."

I cracked my right eye and stole a peek. The handsome guy in a green sweater with gorgeous dark hair had all the tell-tale signs of a fully blooming blush colouring his cheeks. Too cute.

He cleared his throat and stretched out his neck to look through the window on my left. "In a minute, we'll be heading toward the runway."

"And that's where the fun begins, right?"

Each passing minute took me further away from my living hell, and closer to what I hoped – and needed – to be my newly promised beginning.

He shrugged effortlessly. "For some. Most will go to sleep, this being a red-eye and all."

"Don't let me stop you." I rested my head against the wall of the plane. The coolness seeped into my burning left cheek.

"I'm a night owl by nature, so I'll just enjoy the quiet hum of the dim cabin and catch up on some reading." He tapped the pouch in front of him where a thick brick of a novel was snuggly tucked in. "It's *Death by Black Hole,* by Neil deGrasse Tyson. It's a real page turner."

It suited him as it looked like high-level nerdy reading material. Once a nerd, always a nerd it seemed. I shook my head and inhaled sharply while covering my chest. The ache was slowly diminishing, but it hadn't gone away completely. The quick breath proved that.

"Are you sure you're okay, Iris?"

Incredulously, I stared open-mouthed, my eyes widening in response, and he did the same.

"Iris Charbonneau! That's who you are." He snapped his fingers and mumbled as if he had been just as surprised at knowing my name as I was hearing it roll off his lips. "From St. Jude's."

Guess he remembered. Fuck me and my peer-pressure filled high school years.

"Holden deLauer? Does that name ring a bell?"

A rush of regret blew threw me. It came like a slap across the face. Physics class, tenth grade year, some ten years ago. The nerdy dweeb who knew all the answers and was a nasty combo of both a brown noser and the teacher's pet. Didn't help that he was two years younger than the rest of us. Holden had been taunted by me and tormented by my group, until I was sent to yet another foster home at the end of the year.

"I thought you looked familiar." A smidgen of surprise laced the tip of his tongue, not sure if it more or less mirrored what I was experiencing.

"Yeah." Sure, I wasn't the nicest kid in class, but I also wasn't the meanest. Far from it. I only hurt with taunts and jeers, never in the physical sense. Sadly, my gang was responsible for those. "Small world, isn't it?"

"It gets smaller every day." His jovial attitude had marred a touch, but not as much as I suspected it would've. Or should've.

From the side of my eye, I glanced at my former classmate. Why was he not curling his lip in disgust? Why was he being kind and sweet? By all rights, he should be rude and mean; I certainly had been. What was his game plan here?

He shifted as the plane paused in final preparations for takeoff, pushing his back into the seat.

"I suppose I should warn you, in case you don't remember, how I ramble too much and, what was it again? I'm a know-it-all? I may fill your head with useless facts."

Fuck me. He hadn't forgotten a thing. Clearly, this was his plan – make me remember all the bad things I'd done to him. It was going to be a long, painful flight.

"However, if it gets to be too much, please just tell me." He cleared his throat and tossed a quick glance in my direction. His features softened. "We're both grown ups now, and I hope we can be civil towards each other."

Although his voice was soothing, my heart was pounding too erratically, and my blood pressure had to be through the roof, a mixture bound to keep me awake for the duration of the flight without idle chit-chat of recalling all the stupid shit I did years ago. "Fair enough."

"If my memory is correct, you were always one for speaking your mind."

I cringed and turned away. Looked like things have flipped. Now he was the one being direct, and I was cowering.

However, he carried on. "But high school was a long time ago. It's water under the bridge and all that. I'm sure you've matured, settled into your life, and grown up. I know I sure have."

"Yeah, my high school years are far behind me."

High school was the highlight for most people, excluding myself. I was a major shithead likely because I was treated as such. A vicious cycle of nastiness that only intensified until I ran away from that problem and dropped out of high school mid way through grade eleven to move out on my own.

A new ache pinpricked my heart for having been such a punk back in the day.

"But bygones be bygones." He shrugged, and a weak smile filled his face. "Catch me up on the 411 with you."

"No one uses that phrase anymore." I held back a sharp eye roll.

"Point to you. Are you heading to Vancouver, or continuing on to Victoria?"

The plane started moving and through closed eyes, I breathed in deeply. "Even beyond that. A little village on the west coast called Cheshire Bay."

"Never heard of it but visiting anything with a bay in its name sounds nice."

I nodded in agreement and lifted a shoulder. "I'm moving there to lie low for a bit." And that was more information spoken aloud than I'd wanted to share. Blinking away my stupidity at the verbal diarrhea, I scanned his unadorned hand. No ring, no tan line from a ring. Perhaps he was as single as I was. "Married? Kids?"

"At my age?" He covered a cough, and quickly turned away.

Sometimes I felt like I'd experienced more life at twenty-four, and most days, I felt way older than it too.

"Is Vancouver your home now?"

Whatever it took to keep him talking. The melodic effect from his voice calmed my heart and steadied my breathing.

"Actually, I'm making a connection in YVR, that's code for Vancouver."

"I'm aware of what YVR stands for. I've been on social media."

"Yeah, I suppose." He gave me a judgemental once over. "Likely quite popular too."

My internet popularity did not rival that of my high school years, good, bad, or otherwise. I never posted anything, and what would be the point? It was all smoke and mirrors. Nobody was honest on the internet, and if you were, no one cared. No one at all.

"Anyway, I'm moving to Victoria. I'm expected to be at the university first thing Monday morning for a prestigious position within the university."

I gave him a steely-eyed glance. He was younger than me *and* he had a solid job? I needed more clarification. "You'll be working there?"

"Yes, ma'am." After a quick wink, Holden pointed out the window. "Oh, we're moving to the runway now."

This time, I truly opened my eyes to him, rather than a passing glance, and the view was not disappointing. Dark hair and dark green eyes, but the kind that held more sincerity in them than anything frightening. "What should I expect?"

"Well, we'll advance up the line until it's our turn. After that, we'll pull out onto the runaway where it will feel like we're parking but we're not really. The pilots are doing their thing and before you know it, we'll be speeding down the runaway until we lift off." A smile spread over his face.

"What does that feel like?"

"Amazing." A wave of serenity settled over him. Clearly, he was not bothered by flying. "It gets this little lift, and you feel a wave of butterflies in the pit of your stomach." His hands tickled his mid-section. "Like when you go over a bump too fast."

That helped even if I didn't like the sensation.

"You'll also get pushed back into your seat, but only until we reach cruising speed. Then you can move a little easier. Takeoffs are my favourite."

I wasn't sure how to prepare for all of what he said, so I tightened my body in anticipation. Inhaling sharply, I held my breath if for no other reason than to try and control my heartrate. Despite his soothing inflections, my heart suddenly pounded faster than if I'd run away from an overbearing foster father.

"Are you frightened?"

Slowly, I shook my head and snorted out my breath, sounding like a fire-breathing dragon. "Flying is the least of my concerns."

Instead, my thoughts turned to my so-called friends.

Would they miss me? Unlikely.

Did they even notice I had left? Doubtful. I hadn't seen hide nor hair of them since the accident.

It had been seven long, painful days since my violent awakening, only to learn that in my most desperate hour, I had once again failed and was truly alone.

Chapter Three

The plane engines roared to power and with the burst, I was sucked back into my seat as we raced down the runway at full throttle. A heartbeat later, we were in the air, going over the metaphorical speed bump, and a fresh wave of butterflies fluttered in my gut. The sensation was enough to put a temporary smile on my face.

"See, it's not so bad. And it only lasts a few seconds."

And it wasn't. I enjoyed the internal tickles and seeing the roadways of Toronto outlined in the glow of orange; the streetlights getting smaller the higher we climbed. The height wasn't as bad as I'd predicted, and I found myself breathing a little easier. Overall, the view was truly quite spectacular.

My exhale was quiet, and I felt as light as a bird. "You were saying?"

"That it's not so bad."

I laughed and tipped my head back further while

allowing the blood to flow back into my ghost-white hands.

As Holden weighed whatever he was going to share, I took the opportunity to really check him out. Long gone were the thick glasses and scraggly monkey arms he had yet to grow into. Instead, he'd filled out nicely, broad shoulders and, well, normal-length arms. He was clean cut, with a preppy hairstyle parted on the side and his floppy waves long since trimmed and tamed. His face was devoid of facial hair, as if he'd shaved five minutes before stepping on the plane, or maybe it never really grew in. The dark green sweater was a nice cable variety, clearly not from the sale rack at Walmart. It had a more luxurious sheen to it, like it was ripe for a snuggle and wouldn't rough up the cheeks, and his jeans were free of holes. Probably paid more for those two articles of clothing than all the belongings I had cost in total.

But it was his eyes which commanded most of my attention. I'd never before seen a shade of green that hue. It wasn't bright, or dull, but like a dark moss colour. Almost as soothing to look into as it was to hear the soft inflections in his voice.

Holden cleared his throat, and I shook myself free from whatever ghost of a daydream had settled over me.

The plane felt as though it were leveling out and tipping forward, and I quickly looked out the window for confirmation of how high we were. Everything was dark, and no landmarks were visible. Flying was really something.

I blinked a couple of times and focused again on the man beside me. I could sit in arrested silence, like I pretty had over the past week, or I could attempt to swallow a teensy bit of my remaining pride and engage in small talk.

"Tell about this *prestigious* job waiting for you. How'd you get it?"

Like I'd asked the stupidest question, he responded with a trite reply, but a smug smirk. "Hard work, dedication."

"Have you graduated from university?" I inhaled sharply as we pitched forward.

Back in the day, and one of the reasons Holden was picked on was because he was two years younger than we were, all thanks to his incredibly high IQ. He was light years ahead of us and likely started post-secondary ages ahead of the rest of our peers too.

"Yes."

Curiosity overtook me. "When?"

"Got my master's at twenty-one."

"No shit." My eyes widened.

Inside though, my mind was reeling. Smart didn't even begin to appropriately describe him. Holden was a god-damn genius. By the time I was twenty-one, I was broken and homeless. For the first time.

"What do you do?" No doubt, he went into a field where he could put those brain cells to good use. "Wait, let me guess, Mr. Smarty-pants." I said it playfully, although there may have been a hint of green underscoring the words.

"This could be fun." A self-satisfied smile spread from cheek to cheek.

"Hmm... how about..." My finger tapped my dry bottom lip in desperate need of a lip gloss swipe, but since I was without, I gave them a quick lick. "A teacher? You're going to be a professor?"

The grin deepened and showed perfectly straight teeth. Someone had good dental coverage. "Not even in the same field. And nothing I'd ever pursue."

"Really? Interesting." I perused a mental catalog of university classes, my brain mostly empty because having never explored the remote possibilities of a post-secondary education, I wasn't sure what there were for options besides the obvious. "Doctor?"

He shook his head, and relief washed over me. Had he been in the field, our conversations would cease. Immediately. I'd seen enough shrinks and emergency room doctors to distrust most medical professionals.

"Lawyer?" Can you get a master's in law? When he gave me a negative, I tapped my lip again and tried my best to look cute and in deep thought. I even tipped my head to the side for good measure. "Engineer?"

"Now you're getting closer, but I'll help you out since it takes most people a long time to guess."

Did he need to be so egotistical?

"Astrophysics."

"Astrophysics?" It sounded ultra-nerdy, and totally up his alley. "Like rocket scientist shit?"

"Without the shit." But he laughed regardless, and his voice sped as he spoke. "I've been studying astronomy since I was a child, but it evolved into a deeper study of the long wavelengths emitted from pulsars. I was working as part of the Canadian Institute for Theoretical Astrophysics team and just over a year ago, we detected a Fast Radio Burst from a galactic magnetar."

My eyes widened as he spoke in foreign terms. Most of what he just said went right over my head. Too many big words for dumb ole me.

"There I go again. Spewing out randomness. Let me explain it in layman's terms."

"It's all good." There was no need to be talked down to, as much as it was great to see someone so excited for their field of work. In my job, there was nothing exciting about serving food and being yelled at because someone's eggs were over easy instead of sunny side up.

"Do you know what ARO is?"

"Should I?" I twisted a little, putting my back toward the window.

"Probably not, most don't." He shrugged like it was no bid deal; that he'd dealt with this kind of thing all the time. "It's the Algonquin Radio Observatory?"

I shook my head.

"Six hours north of Toronto?"

"I pretty much only know Toronto. You want great takeout, I'm your gal. You asking where things are outside the GTO, you've lost me."

The only tourist information I could provide was the location of Canada's Wonderland, not that I ever went. Whatever the ARO was, I knew zilch about it. But it was great to see him practically jumping up and down in his seat with enthusiasm.

"Fair enough." He inhaled and relaxed his shoulders. "Anyway, after ARO, I got accepted for a prestigious placement at the observatory on the island to expand on my research, but it's just temporary. My big plan is to go to JPL in the next two years."

I didn't know what any of that was, but evident from the large smile stretching out, it was a big deal to him. Bigger than big. "Do all your career aspirations come in weird letter combinations?"

Something akin to a snort rolled out. "No. Well, yes, maybe. JPL is the Jet Propulsion Lab in California. It's more focused on spacecraft, so it would be a small career switch from astronomy, but I have the degrees to back it up."

"Wow. You really know your shit."

"Maybe." A faint blush tickled the edges of his cheeks. "The university seems to see it that way too."

Lucky for him, and deep down, I was happy in a way. Hopefully he was free of the assholes who'd picked on him. Like me. "I know nothing about the stars, aside from what they taught us in school, which really wasn't much."

"No, they don't get too in-depth, that's for sure. They give you just enough to say there, we taught you sky science, but it's minimal at best. A joke really." He shook his head and gazed upon the book in the pocket.

"Next time we cross paths, if it's nighttime, point me out a few star systems, I want to sound smart when I speak of them. Like that famous one. The, uh, big dipper." I snapped my finger when the name finally came to me.

"That's a constellation, not a star system."

I shrugged a shoulder and gave my sweetest smile. "And there went that." But I laughed. Sounding smart and being smart were two completely different things. "What about the places they talk about on Star Wars?"

"Total fantasy, but if you come to the observatory, I'd be happy to show you a bunch of stars. It'll change your whole outlook on the world."

Mission impossible. I cocked my eyebrow. "I highly doubt that."

"We'll see." He turned to the flight attendant when she stopped beside our row with her cart. "I'll take a Coke, please. Iris, what do you want?"

"Umm…" What I wanted was something strong, like a

fireball whiskey, but after what happened a week ago, it was best to give it a pass. "A Coke is fine."

I unfolded the tray and set my drink and cookie down, as Holden did the same.

"Tell me, Iris, what's your story? What have you been up to since the good ole days of St. Jude's?"

I took a sip of the dark cola, allowing the carbonation to bubble and burn on my tongue. After a pensive moment of white knuckling my drink, I set it back down and tore open the package of cookies. "I have no story."

"Right." He drawled out the word. "Everyone has a story."

Pulling out my cookie and sending crumbs everywhere, I ripped myself away from the scrutiny. Not everything needed to be shared. I wasn't an open book. In fact, I was so closed, the key to the lock holding it shut was lost. It was better that way.

"We have tons of time, and you have a captive audience. My sister says I'm a good listener, and the best part is, I never interrupt." A serious expression filled his face. "Besides, if you talk, then I won't be the one talking your ear off."

My gaze fell to the tome in front of him. "Didn't you bring a book?"

"Actually, I had plans to stare out the window for the duration of the flight and see what stars were visible. Up until you arrived, I thought I was sitting alone."

I had grabbed a last minute fair, snagging what the check-in lady said was one of the last seats on the flight. "Why didn't you book the window seat then?"

He shrugged and scanned the airplane. "I honestly didn't think a flight leaving Toronto at midnight and flying across the country would be so full."

I didn't either, which was why I chose to run to the airport at that time, foolishly hoping someone would stop me. Or at the very least, show up and try.

A dull ache spread across my chest and a lump formed in the back of my throat. It sucked being unloved and unwanted, and the loneliness once again bit me in the ass. To try and swallow the bitterness away, I took another sip of my Coke and turned my pained focus to the view out the window.

Speckles of orange and yellow lights dotted the landscape beneath me. Wherever we were, we were high up, and each minute took me further away from the past and toward an unknown future.

After a few cities or town had sailed underneath me, I twisted around in my seat to face Holden. "You said you're the talkative one." A weak smile spread from cheek to cheek. "So, give me the 411 on who Holden is now since I didn't bring anything to keep me entertained."

"Thought you said that phrase was obsolete?" He laughed as he chased his cookie down with the last of his soft drink.

"Fair enough." I couldn't help the hint of a grin.

He shifted in his seat and stretched out his legs under the limited space in front of him. "Let's make it interesting. Do you like twenty questions?"

"Only if I do the asking." My personal life was all mine to keep locked away.

"Nah, it's only fun if we both play." He turned to the passenger across the row. "Hey, buddy. Playing a game over here. What's your favourite colour?"

"Yellow," he deadpanned and reached into the pocket in front of him to pull out the inflight magazine.

Holden returned to my full attention with a broad smile and a sparkle in his eyes. "See, it's not hard. You can even ask first."

A smile was impossible to not return. "Fine. Question one – favourite colour?"

"Green."

"All greens, or any in particular?"

"Is that your second question?"

I pursed my lips together and moved them from side to side. "Sure. That can be my second."

"Fair enough. Bright green."

"Like florescent?"

"Like the colour of the grass after a fresh mowing as the tree branches eclipse the setting sun."

"Wow, that's quite descriptive." I nibbled on my stale

cookie, while looking forward to baking a fresh batch when I got to my destination. "Where did you live to have that kind of grass?"

"Richmond Hill." He nudged me and winked. "See, you're already up to four questions, and it wasn't too painful, was it?"

I counted his own questions and he'd already asked *me* two, and they weren't even personal questions as I'd feared. Rather than answer and chew up my remaining sixteen questions, I shook my head.

"Now I've got you thinking." He gently waved a pointed finger in my direction.

"Yes, you have. I'll have to debate for a minute."

The overhead lights dimmed further and the mood in the cabin changed as well. The low murmurs disappeared.

"Cruising speed commences, and the passengers drift off to sleep. Less than five hours to go." It almost sounded happy, like he was going to enjoy the next few hours.

How did a mere whisper incite a flurry of butterflies in my gut? "Are you really going to stay awake the whole flight?"

"Five," he answered without skipping a beat as he raised his hand and wiggled his fingers and thumb. "And yes, I'm a night-owl by nature. I start getting tired as the sun rises."

He didn't look the least bit sleepy either. Rather, it seemed like he downed an entire can of Red-Bull and was twitching from the energy he couldn't run off. I, on the other hand, felt a wave of light sleep drift over me. Now that I had done my metaphorical running, there wasn't anything left to do but ride it out.

Cheshire Bay was still a forty-five minute flight from Victoria, and even that was still a good hour flight from Vancouver. It would be close to supper time before I finally arrived at Amber's. The mere thought of all the travelling that still lay ahead caused a yawn to roll out, and I hurried to cover my mouth.

"If you are tired, just go to sleep. I swear I won't be offended." His left knee nudged my right one. "Much."

"Well, you do have a nice soothing voice. You'd be able to knock me right out." But I wasn't going to sleep, not without my wallet firmly tucked under my arm where I'd feel the slightest movement if someone tried to take it. Sleep could wait.

* * *

Like everything else in my life, waiting wasn't going to happen.

"What the–"

Holden's hand was wrapped around my arm, shaking me. "You were mumbling. Pretty loud, I may add."

I slapped my hands to my face to wake myself up. I

knew better than to fall asleep, at least here. How hard was it to stay awake and wait until I was at Amber's? It was only another eighteen hours. Nothing to it. I blinked and forced my eyes open for a heartbeat to get some fresh air.

I hadn't meant to doze off. How rude. Pretty sure he was talking about something above my intelligence level, which was probably why I drifted. "Where are we?"

He flipped through the screen on the back of the seat. "Over North Dakota."

"Seriously?" I had to have heard incorrectly. How could we be in US airspace? This was a domestic flight. "How long?"

"Were you out?" Holden finished my thought as I yawned. "A couple of hours. We're almost halfway to Vancouver."

"But we're in the US."

"Temporarily. It's the shortest route."

I didn't understand and shook my head. "What? How?"

"Our flight path may actually spend most of its time over the US. There's a lot of smoke from the forest fires in the west, so we'll have to try and avoid them."

"Flying through smoke is bad?"

He nodded. "Very much so."

The plane jumped, and I sprang my hand out to grab hold of the arm rest.

"Just a little turbulence." The statement was said as if it

were no big deal, but I disagreed.

The plane bounced a lot, and for once I was glad I was buckled in tight.

"Are you hungry?" He pointed to the pocket in front of me. "They came by with snacks, and I hope you don't mind but I picked a few out for you and stuffed them in there. You're not allergic to anything?"

"Nope. One of the lucky ones, I suppose." As I reached for the pocket, my left sleeve caught on the armrest and exposed my forearm. Alone, this wouldn't have been a big deal, but...

There was no mistaking the wide-eye gaze from Holden as he spotted the tiger-stripes of scarring across the inside of my forearm. The most recent marks were still red and raw; the thick, gnarly scab a testament to its newness.

My face heated, and I yanked my sweater sleeve down over my palm. "Thanks for the snacks. What do I owe you?"

I tore open the nosiest plastic bag ever made as my cheeks continued to burn.

"Nothing."

"I can pay my own way." I pulled out my wallet and dug through the few bills, handing him a five.

"I said don't worry." He pushed my hand away. "Besides, that barely covers the cookies."

I put the five away and flabbergasted at the cost of a couple bags of cheap, dried out munchies, handed him a ten.

"It's already taken care of."

Hesitantly, I pocketed the money. "Well, thank you. That wasn't necessary."

"It's not a problem." Holden took a sip of his water and slipped it back into the pocket in front of him. "There is one thing you can do, if you want to pay me back."

"Oh no. I'm not into paying back with favours." I moved as close to the window as possible.

Holden pulled back in disgust, putting more space between us. His brows furrowed tightly together. "Wow. Who said anything about that?"

"Force of … Well… Never mind."

Keeping my gaze focused out the window into the void of darkness, I munched on the dry brownie while forcing myself to swallow it down. Without looking at Holden, I reached for the bottle of water and uncapped it, taking a quick swig.

The minutes ticked by in utter silence, and it seemed even the plane itself had a quiet hum. An awkward wedge of tension had pounded between us; I leaned as far away from Holden as I could. In response, he also pushed away like I was diseased; he was practically in the aisle.

I took a sharp breath. "What's the one thing I can do?"

"I just want to ask one question."

"Just one?" I lifted a finger to solidify my point. "As part of the twenty questions game?"

"Sure." He nodded to confirm. "Just one. Promise."

I finished my water bottle and tucked it back into the pocket. Holden stared at my covered wrist, which I pulled close to my chest.

"For the record," my voice turned smug and defensive. "I know what you're thinking and you're wrong. I don't need help. It's superficial."

At least the first time, and I was discharged after a consult with the resident psychologist. However, my file was marked. The next visit, they were a bit blunter, and yet, in a way, kinder. That incident required four stitches, but again, I hadn't done any real damage as once again I'd missed the artery. Each attempt was closer, but never good enough. However, I couldn't recall with much clarity the last attempt, just bits and pieces.

Holden reached into the pocket in front of him and took a drink from his water bottle.

"I'm not crazy." If I repeated the phrase enough, it should come true.

Because I wasn't. Crazy people didn't know what they were doing. I did. It was all planned out. It wasn't my fault if it didn't go the way it was intended. That didn't make me crazy. All it did was reveal the truth. Again. No matter what I did, I failed. Horribly.

He pointed at my water. "You should have another sip."

"It's empty."

"Excuse me." Holden unbuckled and walked to the front of the plane.

A sting of rejection kicked me in the ass. My weak attempt to bare a tiny portion of my soul was foiled. A heavy weight sagged my shoulders, and I leaned into the depths of my seat, putting my hand over my aching chest.

My seat mate returned and handed me another room temperature water bottle, tucking another into my seat pocket.

I narrowed my eyes slightly and smiled weakly. "Thank you."

"Flying can make a person dehydrated. Best to keep drinking."

I half expected him to turn away and either fiddle with the screen or pull his book out and read. Ignoring me, like so many others had, would've been more on par. Instead, after he buckled in, he faced me, narrowing the gap that had formed.

"Can I ask one of my twenty questions now?" Genuine concern settled over him, his features softening with each passing breath. He looked deep into my eyes, but he didn't wait for me to answer. "How can I help you?"

Chapter Four

ever in my life had anyone asked what I needed, and I was gutted for a respectable answer. When my few friends learned of my failed suicide attempts, they stopped talking to me, at least about real things. They no longer talked about anything personal, rather conversations turned to weather or the latest movie or *OMG, what is she wearing*? Once, I overheard a friend say if she brought up the suicide attempt, she was afraid it'd give me more ideas. As if. Trust me, I had plenty.

Deep down I should've been happy they wanted me to stick around, but instead it made me pull away even more. They didn't understand. We had nothing in common. They had everything they ever wanted, and they took it all for granted. I had lived in my car for most of my adult life, up until a week ago, and I had to fight for everything in my possession, which sadly wasn't much anymore. It was all in the bag stashed under the seat in front of me, with an additional bag in cargo. A whole life crammed into two bags. There wasn't anything worth fighting for.

"It's okay, you don't need to talk about it, if you don't want to." Holden didn't break eye contact. "And I can't say I've been there, because I don't know what you've gone through or whatever it is you're currently going through, but back in high school, I too, struggled with depression, and believe me, suicide was a thought that had crossed my mind."

An even bigger lump formed in my throat. "Because of my group?"

"Not your group. Not really. But they didn't help." He shook his head. "In grade eleven, it was a new group, and they were mean. Really mean. My parents didn't want to move, wanted me to fight for my place since I was entitled to be there just as much as they were. And things got worse, but I'll spare you the details." He picked at the ribbing on his sweater. "However, since I feel I can share this with you, one day, while riding my bike home alone from school, I considered driving into oncoming traffic."

"What stopped you?" My voice lowered to a bare whisper, and I nearly regretted the words coming out because if someone asked me, I don't know if there would've been anything to have stopped me aside from my insane inability to take my life properly.

"I really wish I had an answer for you. Mostly, I realised

I didn't want to go. I knew my parents and sister would be crushed, and I hoped things would get better. Corny, right?"

I broke contact and flipped my gaze over to the screen. It flashed an updated flight image. We were over Canadian soil once again.

Holden carried on. "I know now that I was just sad and hurting because I felt so all alone. That kind of solitude was all consuming."

Hearing the world *alone,* I searched his face. He understood and was telling the truth; that depth of loneliness was rare, and it put you in a special club.

"I know now, and perhaps deep down I sort of knew then, but there was much to live for and still is. I just needed to get a fresh perspective on things, and make it through the day, hour by hour, sometimes even minute by minute. What I found helped me at least, as awkward and painful as it was, was talking to people about my feelings. I talked to the school counsellor and made some changes in my life. I stepped outside my comfort zone, big time and, this probably won't surprise you, I started an astronomy club at school, fueling my passion. However, part of that requirement was leading and teaching a group of eager beavers. Let me tell you, I learned to respect my teachers a heck of a lot more." He chuckled lightly and tipped his head back. "Want to hear something funny?"

I didn't get a chance to agree or disagree.

"If you can believe it, the biggest jock in school joined. He wanted to learn everything about the constellations as he was trying to impress a nerdy girl he desperately wanted to date."

I rolled my eyes, but Holden carried on.

"But it was more than that. That jock? We became fast friends, and in a way, he became my bodyguard. After one unfortunate incident where my arm was broken by a bully, and my new friend taught that guy a lesson, no one touched me. Jeremy became my biggest fan, as much as I was his. He clapped the loudest at the awards and graduation ceremonies, and I cheered the hardest at his games."

"Sounds like you either fell in love or you're the best of friends." A sardonic laugh escaped.

"The absolute best of friends." He smiled, the kind that suggested a warm memory was tickling his brain. "He now plays for the NFL, no surprise there as he is a formidable wide receiver, but we get together at least once a month to drink beers and stare at the stars."

My curiosity was piqued as to who this nameless guy was, even though I didn't follow any football. Sports weren't an activity I had a remote interest in.

"You're lucky."

"How so?"

"You have friends."

The statement hung in the air between us as the plane

bounced once again with turbulence – the water in my bottle sloshed around violently.

"Tell you what." Holden stuck out his left hand, palm side up when the plane leveled out. "From now on, I promise I will always be your friend. You will never be alone."

I cocked an eyebrow and stared at his open, yet empty hand. "I didn't make the comment so you'd have pity on me. It was off the cuff."

"And I swear it's not pity, just an understanding of your truth within the words. You don't have to be alone, Iris. We'll both be on the island. Besides, I have selfish interests. It'd be nice to have someone to visit once in a while." He wiggled his fingers.

"You remember me, right? The mean girl who picked on you and made sure you had a rough year. Seriously, you can find better friends."

Why I needed to remind him of my foul behaviour was beyond understanding. Here was a decent guy, a damn smart guy, offering me a literal hand in friendship, and I was pushing him away. Idiocy clearly ran in my veins.

The plane shifted again, and the fasten seatbelt came on. My eyes widened as my heart palpitated wildly in my chest. These constant jumps from the plane were unnerving.

The flight attendant walked quickly by with an open bag so passengers could dispose of their garbage.

Holden spoke and grabbed my attention. "Honestly, I

think you've grown up. I know I have. Besides, I don't hold grudges."

"Seriously?" How was that possible? The list of people I hoped to never cross paths again was a mile long.

"Oh wait, you're not still friends with Adam, Jordan, and Mel, are you?" He rescinded his hand and his left eyebrow lifted, but there was a hint of a grin trying to peek out.

I shook my head. Adam was the ringleader of our group, a total badass, and also a part-time lover. "After I left St. Jude's, we fell out of touch. Probably just as well. Last I heard, Jordan had served time in jail."

"For what?"

I shrugged, not knowing all the details because I really wasn't surprised and couldn't care less. "Robbery?"

"Wow."

"Great crowd I ran with, eh?" At the time, I'd even thought they were grade-A friends.

"We all learn from our mistakes, otherwise what's the point?"

I stared at Holden, assessing his words and facial expressions. High school life was rough for just about everybody, but for him, two years younger than his peers, it had to have been a nightmare. Bullies and tormentors galore.

Sadly, I had been a small part of his personal hell. "I'm so sorry."

His tongue wetted his lips, and then he laughed.

"Whatever for?"

"For that year. For being less than kind to you. You didn't deserve the nightmare you lived through." I tipped my head to the side. "I wasn't very nice, and looking back, I know that. I think I even knew that then, but peer pressure and all. It was ..."

Did he really need to know high school was a form of hell for me too? Not likely. Not that it was an excuse, but I was a product of my environment, something which took me a long time to break out of. At least partially. Leaving Toronto was hopefully going to nail that coffin closed.

"Water under the bridge. Honestly. I'd long since forgiven you."

I blinked and tried to figure him out. Clearly, Holden was a better person than I would ever be. Forgiveness was not something I doled out. Not now, not ever. Hurt ran deeper in my veins than any visible scar.

But Holden? How was it possible that? He was just–

The plane violently shifted again, and a male voice cut through the quiet atmosphere over the PA. "Cabin crew, please be seated."

Chapter Five

n a flash, the cabin crew disappeared from the aisles.

"Is this normal?" I tried to hide the fear creeping into the panic edges of my pitch.

Holden nodded. "Oh yeah. They'll get pockets of bad air, but it's just safer if everyone is in their seats for a short spell."

The cabin lights remained dim, but the passengers stirred, and the mumbles increased as the plane continued to bounce through the air.

It was hard to hold a conversation. Every time I went to speak, the plane dipped, or did whatever it was when it hit a so-called *pocket of air*. I didn't understand what turbulence was, but I wasn't a fan of it. All my life, I'd avoided watching movies about airplanes for just this reason.

The plane jumped again, a little more violently than previous bumps.

I reached for Holden's hand. Right now, I needed the contact.

He didn't let me down and placed his other hand on top of mine. "It'll be okay."

"This... seems... wrong."

"Nah. It has to do with the mountain air and currents and jet streams. Most likely, the pilot is adjusting the speed and trying to climb above. It'll be smooth soon, you'll see."

I nodded, hoping he was correct in his blasé explanation. It sure didn't feel like we were rising.

The plane shook again, and I was thrust against the restraints of my seatbelt. My free hand white-knuckled the hand rest as I inhaled sharply to control my breathing. It was crazy, but I refused to look out the window. Some irrational part of my brain worried the ground was racing up towards us and the rational part didn't want confirmation.

"Ladies and Gentlemen," a calm male voice spoke over the PA system again. "We're going to be making an unscheduled stop in Calgary. Cabin crew prepare for imminent landing."

We looked at the screen on the head rest. The plane's altitude was dropping, as was my stomach when the plane pitched slightly.

"Is that... normal?"

Holden shrugged, and I took his lack of an answer as a no. Planes don't make unscheduled stops.

Something was up. Something was definitely up.

A few minutes after the announcement, the flight attendant roamed the aisles, taking away the remaining trash and ensuring trays were in their upright and locked positions.

"Excuse me," I asked as the one flight attendant walked by.

"Yes." If she was worried, her relaxed demeanour betrayed that. She was the poster child of serenity.

"What happens when we land in Calgary?"

"We wait."

"That's it?"

"That's all I've been told." She backed down the aisle, stopping every couple of feet.

I searched Holden's face, but he too remained calm and composed. "You're not bothered by this?"

"Nah. It happens."

I shook my head. "Like all the time?"

"No, not always. But it's better to land than take a chance."

A hard statement to disagree with. Despite my best efforts, I was unable to keep the panic out of my voice. "So what do we do?"

"Most likely, if it's going to be a wait of a couple of hours, we'll sit on the tarmac, and wait for clearance to take off again, especially if it's just weather related. The storm will pass, and we'll be on our way."

There was a hesitation on the tip of his tongue.

"But..."

He searched to see if anyone was listening and lowered his voice as he twisted closer to me. "If it's mechanical, we'll deplane at an available gate, and they'll unload the passengers and put everyone onto a new plane. They'll transfer the luggage over."

Although I didn't know Holden well enough to know any of his tics, I understood people as a general rule. He was holding something back; it was there in the reserved way he spoke and the way he put a bit of space between us, but it was the way he refused eye contact that sounded the alarms.

I waited and let go of his hand, opening and closing it to bring back the blood flow. "Or?"

"Or, if this is going to be a much longer wait, we'll deplane, grab our luggage, and need to rebook with the airline onto a different flight. That seems like a worse case scenario and would mean there's something huge going on. Personally, I think it's just weather related, and we'll be parking until it passes."

"Is that all?" I deadpanned. "Can't we fly above the clouds?"

"There's only so high we can go, and the mountain range is already a tough airspace."

"What do you think's going to happen?" I looked into the depths of his eyes. It seemed like he'd travelled on enough flights to know. "Answer honestly, I can handle bad news."

Without skipping a beat, he answered solemnly. "I think we'll be eating stale cookies for a few hours in Calgary."

Chapter Six

It was pushing three in the morning when our plane taxied up to the gate and opened the doors, spilling the weary passengers out into the waiting area of the airport. So much for sitting on the tarmac and waiting. I hated how Holden was right.

The smoke blowing in from the out of control forest fires throughout the lower British Columbia mainland and northwestern USA were causing massive flight delays. The forestry services declared multiple no fly zones so they could extinguish and control the fires.

According to the ticket agent at the airline check-in, there were no flights into BC. We just had to sit, wait, and be patient. A virtue I'd never had.

Holden was waiting just beyond the ticketing counter when I walked toward him. "Any luck?"

"No." I sighed. At least I was a long way from Toronto,

but I wasn't anywhere near my intended destination, maybe half-way. "All flights are grounded. She said all should be good in a couple of days and gave me a list of nearby hotels to stay at."

Holden rolled his eyes. "That's great. I'm supposed to be at the university on Monday morning."

Which was just over forty-eight hours away. Sticking around for a fight would be a waste of time, although there wasn't much he could do.

"Have you considered taking a bus?"

"Like the big greyhounds? No thanks." He shook his head, and shifted his weighted backpack over his shoulder. The straps dug into his sweater. "Have you ever ridden on a bus?"

"Just a yellow bus for school. When I was ten."

"It's like that, but longer. Not any fun and an absolute last case scenerio. Ugh. I can't just sit around and wait. I have things to do, places to be. People are counting on me to show up." There was a borderline panic in his tone. He spun on his heels and released a loud, painful exhale. "They're unloading the bags onto the carousel. Let's collect our luggage while I think this through."

I followed him past the endless line of airline counters, populated with frustrated and angry passengers, and high-pitched voices. Trying to get a different flight would've been pointless, since all flights heading into the lower BC mainland were cancelled. The flight boards with red *cancelled* all over backed that notion.

Despite the growing crowds from the recently landed arrivals, none of the restaurants and kiosks were open, and therefore, there wasn't any place to grab a hot cup of coffee, something I desperately wanted. I yawned, but considering the hour, I was quite surprised how awake I was.

Holden on the other hand, had the zest of the energizer bunny and had more of a spring in his step than normal people should have at three am.

The carousel started with an awful grinding sound, and the buzzer flashed overhead, sending a current of fresh adrenaline through my body. Any lingering sleep was wiped out in a heartbeat. One by one, bags popped out from behind the rubber door.

"What about a car rental?" I had just scanned the area and spied a few rental agencies.

Lights were on in each of the stations, and the lineups were manageable of only a few people. Less than the plane load of travellers gathered around the baggage claim area.

"I don't know. That's a long drive."

"And why taking the bus would be the better alternative." I winked. "Plus you could read or sleep, and not have to worry about any of this shit."

"Except I get nauseated if I can't see out the front window, so I'll have to reject that idea on the grounds of not wanting to get sick."

"How did you manage on the plane then?"

He tipped his head and pointed to a white, circular patch. "It's a Scopolamine transdermal patch prescribed by my doctor, and since we're now grounded, it's useless."

"Unless you take the bus?"

He pulled the little patch off and walked over to a nearby trash bin. "Problem solved. No bus ride."

"Not really, unless you do decide to rent a car?" The line ups were starting to grow.

Holden reached forward and pulled a giant suitcase off the turning rack and placed it between us. "One down, one to go."

I waited for my lonely checked bag, which had failed to make an appearance so far.

"Do you have a license?" I asked. Maybe that's why he was hesitant.

"Of course." He said it in such a way I nearly took offense.

"Then a car rental is the way to go. You can plug in your final destination in google maps, and boom, it'll get you to Victoria." I didn't see what was so complicated about it.

Now Holden laughed, but I wasn't sure why. "I know how Google maps work."

"Figured." I tipped my head and released a breath.

He gave me a friendly nudge. "You've never caught a

ferry ride, have you?"

"No." I wondered what that had to do with a car rental.

"They're almost as expensive as a flight when you're driving. Might be cheaper to drive to Vancover and fly into Victoria."

"So, you *are* thinking about taking the rental, eh?" I leaned on my left foot and let a playful smirk tease its way across my face.

He scanned the lineup. "Fine. I'm contemplating the idea. I've just never rented a car before. It's a lot of contracts and details."

"It can't be that hard." I spotted my lone, giant suitcase as it birthed onto the baggage claim area. With a bit of a struggle, I lugged it off and hoisted it off the carousel, setting it down with a thump.

His face lit up, and he reached for his second bag, checking to make sure the tag on it was correct. "Nothing like taking home the wrong case."

"That would suck." Considering all my worldly possessions were enclosed in mine.

"That it?" he asked.

"That's it."

He scanned the area, and then focused back on my suitcase. "The rest of your things on a moving truck?"

I laughed, but it may have been due to the late hour. "No." I shook my head. "This is it."

"Oh. Wow." His gaze jumped between my luggage, my backpack, and me, flipping back more times than I could count. "You still need to get to the island, right?"

"Eventually. My cousin's friend is a pilot and will be picking me up."

Holden tipped his head and a half grin showed. "How sweet is that?"

"It's not an on demand thing, he'll just happen to be in Victoria in the morning."

"Well... I'm going to go out on a limb here, but I'm pretty sure you'll need to call and cancel. We're not getting there by morning. Not even if we took a bus." He grimaced with the last word.

Damn it though, he was right. It was foolish to have been so self-centered. Of course, Amber would need to notify her pilot friend as there was no way I was going to be there waiting in a couple of hours. I pulled out my phone and sent a quick text to let her know that at this point in time I had no idea what I was doing, but I was sitting in Calgary trying to figure it out.

"What about you? Don't you have someone to text with your late arrival? Like the university?"

He laughed and stepped away from me for a moment to grab a couple of luggage carts. He added his bags to one, and tossed his backpack on top, then grunted as he put my bag onto a cart.

"What are you carrying? That bag must've cost a fortune to check in."

It was true, but I justified it. I *was* relocating across the country, so I considered it a travel expense. Although, in hindsight, buying it its own seat on the plane may have been cheaper.

When I didn't answer his question, he answered the one I'd asked before. "Since I'm staying temporarily with my grandparents, I'll call them in the morning. They don't do text messages, especially not at–" He checked his watch. "Three seventeen in the morning. They're old school in that regard. They prefer voice to voice over that text mumbo-jumbo."

"Mumbo-jumbo." I repeated and laughed. That was a fun word to say, and not at all sophisticated.

"You know what, and this is going to sound crazy..."

"At this point, anything said at three am will *be* crazy."

"True, but as I was saying." He nudged with his shoulder towards the car rental agencies. "Why don't you come with me?"

"You're serious?"

"As a heart attack." He pushed ahead of me while I stood there with a dumb expression upon my face. I'm pretty sure I didn't even blink. "Come on."

I raced to catch up, and when I did, I pulled him to a stop. "Yeah, I don't think so."

"Are you going to hang out here in the airport and just

wait? That's lunacy."

"Says you, who up until a few minutes ago was thinking the same thing."

"Yeah, but what you said made sense, and besides I need to get to the university. It's not a negotiation, and it's not something I can delay. I have a meeting at eight Monday morning. My whole life I've been waiting for this, and I can't, I won't allow a hiccup like this to derail my future." He leaned against the backpack propped up on his luggage. "Do you really want to stay here and hope for a flight out? You could be with your friends in a few short hours."

"A few hours?" I laughed. "Even I know it takes longer than that to get to Victoria."

He shrugged and pulled out his phone, opening the map app. "Well, would you look at this. You're correct. It's eleven and a half hours to Vancouver International airport, if we didn't stop anywhere along the way."

"See, that's a long drive." I snorted. Three times as long as the flight that only brought me this far.

"We could split the driving into two shifts or four shifts. With the swapping, we could be in Vancouver by late afternoon. It's totally doable."

"Not calling it yvr?" I mocked, but it was late, and I got more sarcastic the tireder I became.

"What do you think? In theory, you could be having dinner with your cousin if we left now."

I hung my head. As easy as he made it sound, there was a giant *no way* coming. "I… can't drive. Well, it's not that I can't, because I know how and all, it's that I… Can't."

The license suspension was still fresh. A week old; a newborn. Too many more weeks to go.

"Oh?" A questioning tone lingered on the tip of his lips and in the rounded upward curve of his brow.

"Yeah. What can I say? I always fuck things up." Seeing Holden's eyes bug out, I covered my mouth. "Sorry. I tend to swear like a trucker, especially when I'm exhausted."

"Well, that does change the method, but the results should still be the same."

"It's all good. Really. I appreciate you asking, and I don't mind hanging out here. I've never been in Calgary before." I spun around and looked for an information kiosk. "Didn't they have an Olympics here or something? I can play tourist and check out these places." From google maps, because there wasn't a lot of money to put behind a tourist adventure.

He tapped his foot as he leaned on his pile of bags. "Is that what you really want to do?"

I rocked on my feet, from the heels to the toes and back again. I didn't know what I really wanted to do. This whole thing was supposed to be easy. Leave everything and everyone behind, hop on the plane, make a transfer flight and wait for Amber's pilot friend to pick me up to take me to a place where

I could figure out what to do. There wasn't supposed to be any detours along the way.

"Listen, I've got this. If you don't mind being a passenger, and maybe a navigator, I don't mind doing the driving. Besides, the company would be nice." He resumed pushing his baggage cart toward the car rental. "Think about it while I make the necessary arrangements."

As we approached the rental agency, the one with the shortest line, he parked his cart. "Can you watch my stuff?"

I nodded, moved my own cart to rest beside his, and sat on the nearby chair. My body was weary, and pangs of hunger roared in the depths of my gut. Before I made any hasty decisions, I needed to eat. Hangry me never made the best choices, not that content me did either, but at least it helped. Sort of.

Rifling through my bag, I pulled out a protein bar and scarfed it down, chasing it with the rest of the room temperature water I had. A quick glance at my phone on the reverse photo side, I pushed at the size of the growing baggage under my eyes. What I really needed, more than food, was a long and restful nap.

Yawning, I straightened my legs, pulled my hair out of the messy bun, and redid it, making myself a little more presentable. I slapped a bit of colour into my cheeks and stretched for as long as it felt comfortable, infusing a little energy into my soul. I'd just yanked the sleeve of my sweatshirt down when Holden walked over.

"Well, that was time consuming, and she really skipped over a lot of the details that I needed to hound her for more information on." He caught his breath. "But I'm all set. A little compact car to whisk me through the mountains and valleys and over to Vancouver. Personally, I would've prefered an SUV or something with a little more space, but that's all they had." He waved the paperwork. "Room for one more, if you're interested?"

"I really shouldn't." I made no effort to rise, and slumped further into the hard-backed plastic chair.

Holden's shoulders rolled in and a solumness filled his face. "Oh. Okay."

"I think it would be best if I hang out here for a bit." I was guaranteed a transfer, which wouldn't cost me a dime. Driving would. With limited funds, I had to choose the cheaper option, even if it was less than ideal.

"I understand." He stuffed the paperwork into his bag.

I reached out to touch his arm. "Thanks for keeping me company on the plane. It was good to catch up with you, and I sure do appreciate you holding my hand during the—" The word escape my brain. "Instability."

"Turbulence."

"Yes. That."

He ran his hands over his face, and looked everywhere and anywhere except at me. "You take care. Call me when you're settled, and we'll plan a get together. I said you'd have a friend in me, and I don't run away from my promises."

I nodded.

"Give me your phone."

I didn't know what else to do, so I handed it over. A ping rang out on his phone.

"Now we're all set." He pocketed it. "I'm serious, give me a call and at the very least, I'll give you a tour of the night skies. You can make a trip out to YYJ, or I can come find you."

It sounded appealing, but deep down, I knew it wasn't going to happen. Once he was out that door, it was over, and we both needed to accept it. Holden was just being nice. Still, I wasn't going to make this any harder than it needed to be.

"Sure thing."

He jerked his cart away, gave me a quick wave, and headed toward the outside loading area. After he was through the doors, a little splinter cracked across my heart.

What the hell was the matter with me? Here was a chance to make amends to the guy I'd wronged all those years ago by keeping him company, and awake, so he could make the drive safely, and I was letting the opportunity walk away. How many times in life do you get a second chance to make things right?

Besides, he was a sweetie and in all honesty, even if he chattered the whole trip, it woud still be more entertaining than being all alone. Wasn't that what this journey was about?

With a jump, I landed on my feet, and pushed my weighted cart as fast as my tired legs could carry me.

I burst through the doors, feverishly scanning the group of people. "Holden, wait."

Chapter Seven

The biggest smile to ever greet me was plastered on Holden's face when I caught up to him in line, ready to board the bus to the car drop off. It was sincere, and its appearance caused a rapid acceleration of my heart.

"Changed your mind?"

"Obviously." I playfully punched him in the shoulder. "Figured you could use a navigator, and I happen to be fantastic at reading maps and giving directions."

"I thought Google was supposed to help me?" He winked and carried my bags onto the transport bus. "But I already appreciate the company."

Arriving at the dark blue car, he placed my heavy suitcase in the trunk and added one of his. I didn't miss the long, lingering glance he sent my way which was warmer than the August breeze and roused a flutter of dragonflies in my gut. Thankfully, the slightly smokey-scented breeze cooled my heated cheeks, as it also wafted stray pieces of my hair across my face. Pushing them off, I tried my best to be alluring. I failed, since he broke the gaze and put his remaining luggage into the backseat, along with our carryon bags.

"Do you mind if we just drive straight for a while?" He'd hopped behind the wheel and buckled in while he stared at the dash as the car came to life.

"No sightseeing stops?" I said with a cheery tone, but I was kidding of course. It was after four am, and there wasn't much to see in the dark.

Leaning into my seat, I fought back a yawn as my body believed it was still two hours ahead, and I'd only managed to sleep a couple of hours tops in the last two days. I wasn't sure how I was going to stay awake for most of the ride.

"I need a coffee first." Holden punched the button on the radio and quickly lowered the volume. "Want one?"

The word *coffee* perked me up since I desperately needed one too. "Do I ever."

"Great. We'll stop there." He pulled in front of a convenience store. "Ever done a road trip?"

I shook my head and followed Holden into the brightly lit interior of the store.

"What we always used to do was a snack run before we start out. You get a max limit of let's say ten bucks, and you load up on junk food. Whatever will get you to the next stop."

"And you don't worry about getting sick?" Since he was

standing by the length of shelves stocked with chocolate bars upon candies upon bags of toffee, it seemed a reasonable thing to question.

"It all depends on what you grab. But you only get two minutes." He scrolled through his phone and set a timer. "And go."

"Are you serious?" My eyes widened.

"You have to be at the checkout in one minute fifty-two seconds." Holden was already over in the chips and salty needs aisle, scanning for an item or two to add to his supplies.

Feeling the time crunch, I dashed over to the cooler and grabbed a small carton of chocolate milk, ran to the coffee station. I needed to be practical, and caffeine was a must.

"One minute twenty-eight seconds."

"Okay, okay." I imagined the seconds ticking by as I pushed the button for a sugar loaded French vanilla beverage which took forever to dispense into the extra-large size cup.

"Fifty-three seconds," Holden called out somewhere behind me.

A coffee and a chocolate milk weren't going to be enough, as I had no idea if we'd be stopping for a breakfast or driving straight until our next fill up, so I quickly scanned around. What my body needed was nourishment. I spied a basket of yellow-green bananas, and yanked one out.

"Twenty-six seconds."

The clock was ticking, and as I raced to the counter first,

I added a Mars bar, and if my math was correct, I still had at least two dollars remaining.

Holden arrived with his hot drink and an arm full of snacks, almost as if a child had been set loose. He dropped his two chocolate bars, a bag of blue gummy fish, a small packet of pringles, a snack size Skittles and his extra-large cup beside mine.

I laughed at the lunacy of his choices, but had to admit, it was fun.

He stared at my choices. "Really? Where I could let the chocolate milk slide, because it has chocolate in its name, the banana is not really junk food worthy."

"It's a treat for me," I said with a wink. "Oh, and I'm paying for this."

"No way."

I grabbed some cash.

He pushed my hand to my wallet, holding it there for a heartbeat longer than necessary.

I thrust the money at the cashier, loving the lopsided smirk peeking from between Holden's lips. "I insist. You paid for the rental, let me get the extras that go with it."

The cashier bagged our order and handed the bag to us, which Holden snapped up in an instant.

"Are you going to be this bossy the whole ride?"

I tipped my head to the side and let a tired smile lazily stretch from ear to ear. "Probably, but you did insist I come with you. So considered yourself warned."

With our two XL coffees in hand, we set off, leaving the Calgary airport behind in our dust. Using Google maps, we managed to escape the city and head out on the open road, but there wasn't much to see in the dark. Too bad, as I would've enjoyed seeing more of the scenery, especially having never been in the Rocky Mountains before.

"Okay, since I apparently insisted you join me," Holden released a light laugh, "then the pressure's on you to help make this ride interesting. So, we can play twenty questions, or you can give me the 411 on you, and then I won't have to guess."

"Are those my two choices?" I let the sweetness from my coffee drink sit on the tip of my tongue.

"Yep. Or the third, less exciting option, is I can talk the whole way and regale you with my finer knowledge of all the interesting places we're going to pass by and not see as we drive on through the mountains in the dark."

"That option can work, then I won't feel like I'm missing anything." I let the cheery and hopeful tone fill the space.

"Not big on sharing, eh?"

I turned away from his gaze. "I may have a tiny bit of issues when it comes to trust, so yeah."

"But you're here with me now?"

"That doesn't mean I'm going to spill all my secrets."

"Not all, but some?" There was a sense of hope in his words.

"Doubtful."

"That's too bad, sometimes secrets can be quite entertaining."

"Or destructive." I deadpanned. Mine were all that way. None of them even remotely exciting.

He made sure the radio was off. "Why don't I go first then? Make it easier."

"You're going to share a secret with me?" We were barely more than acquaintances.

"Sure am. Did you know that I'm typically painfully shy around women?"

I scoffed, holding back a *pfft, please,* and took a drink, trying to hide the noise beneath a cough. "Really? You don't make it a habit of talking to complete strangers everywhere you go?"

"Not at all." He was dead serious. "There was just something about you I guess my subconscious recognized before the rest of my brain clued in as to who you are. Most of the time, I'm happier to just be in my own little world, reading and studying and keeping to myself."

"I can actually understand that." I nodded to the thought. It was easier that way.

"Can you?"

"Why do you sound so surprised?"

He shrugged. "You just seemed like a popular girl back in high school, outgoing and quite vocal."

"I guess I've changed."

"Was it a guy?"

My gaze widened at his question. "What?"

He grimaced. "Sorry, that was out of line. It's just I've heard that sometimes breakups can change a person, make them flip from being who they used to be at the start of things, into someone they never thought they'd be."

"Speaking from experience?"

"Not really. My relationships have been limited, but I am a good listener."

I tried to reign in my soft laugh, but it failed.

"I do listen, believe it or not, it's just that I don't like abbreviated pauses or long gaps in conversations, so I tend to fill the silence to take away the awkward." He took a noisy sip of his drink.

I fought a yawn, and not because I was bored of the conversation, Holden was an interesting guy, but I'd been up for so long that Mr. Sandman was tugging on my eyelids.

"Are you tired?"

"Aren't you?" I countered.

"Not yet." He tore open one of his chocolate bars and tossed the wrapper on the floor behind out seats.

I grabbed it and stuffed it into the bag at my feet, while looking out the window into nothingness. "Tell me about where we are, right now."

"Well, we're on the Trans-Canada Highway. This highway stretches from Vancouver all the way to Nova Scotia."

And for the next thirty minutes, Holden filled the space with information I never knew, and would likely forget. He had a way of talking about facts that actually made it interesting.

However, despite the jolt of caffeine and an overload of sugar, the random knowledge Holden was imparting on me wasn't preventing me from nodding off every so often. I woke and stared at Holden through my half-closed eyes. The soft glow from the awakening skies illuminated the way he'd perfectly blossomed into a damn good-looking guy. A perfectly set jawline, a nose with a tiny upturn on the tip, and long lashes to die for. He covered a yawn and wiped at his eyes.

"Why don't you pull over and get some rest?" My own voice sounded tired and worn. I was tempted to add how dangerous it was to drive while tired, but bit my tongue being that I wasn't exactly a poster child of a perfect driver and rule follower. My suspended license was case in point.

"You know, it's nearly eight already, and I'd be on the flight to Victoria. If things had not detracted from the set plan, I'd be landing by 9:15, and that's when she'd be leaving to pick me up. My plan is to call her in thirty minutes and update her on the situation when we grab some breakfast, stretch, and top up the tank for the rest of the mountain pass. We don't want to be stuck on the side of the road without gas." His words practically fell over top of one another in a big, giant ramble, and he ran a hand through his thick wavy hair, scratching the back of his head before he tipped it from side to side.

"See? You are tired because you didn't even answer my question and none of what you just said made much sense. Why don't you pull over and rest?"

"After I call Grandma, I'll consider your request." He chased back the last of his nursed coffee.

Meanwhile, I took a pretend sip as I'd finished mine about an hour ago, but didn't want to let on. We'd be stopping soon enough.

"Can I change the station?" His finger hovered over the button. "I need something more uplifting than country music. Don't know how much more I can take of breakups and pickup trucks."

"I truly don't care what we listen to as long as it's not death metal." The ex-boyfriend had been a long-time fan, and hearing it only made my skin crawl.

He randomly flipped until he found one that wasn't a talk radio station or country.

"Hey, it's a song about you."

I sighed.

That was just the name of the song, but there was no way it was about me. The Goo Goo Dolls wrote that for some movie and besides, I was no angel, and there was no truth in my lies for the simple reason I never lied to begin with. Still, it was intriguing to watch Holden silently sing along as he head-bobbed in time to the music. Whatever kept him from nodding off was one hundred percent okay with me.

The sun slowly rose behind us, and the skies grew brighter, making it easier to watch for wildlife on the side of the roads. It also made the giant, carved out rocks we drove through a borderline point of interest. I'd never seen a such a monstrous rock look like it was split down the middle and a road paved between. I quickly snapped a picture, marveling as we approached.

More importantly though, the rising sun showed the real danger of driving in the mountains. The guard rails alongside the highway were the only thing separating us from a long drop into the valley. That was enough to keep my heart pounding whenever Holden took the turn in what I thought was a little too fast for the curve.

His phone buzzed.

"Aren't you going to check that? That's the twenty-third time it's done that." It was irritating.

"Not while I'm driving. Besides it's likely just my friends who are checking to see if I've landed."

"Nice." I flipped my phone over and stared at a screen

blank with notifications. No one had bothered to reach out.

Thankfully, the voice on the GPS announced we were descending into the valley town of Golden, so I opened the app, ignoring my lingering ache, to see what we were near. Golden was a small dot on the landscape, and the only town for miles.

"Let's stop here." I glanced over at the gas gauge. The compact car was highly fuel efficient, but we still needed to top it up. "This place looks like it has everything we'll need; gas and food."

"An unbeatable combination." He nodded slowly and rested his head on his braced arm.

I knew he was on a deadline to get to Victoria, but it also didn't need to come with sleep deprivation, on top of the time change, which our bodies hadn't yet adapted to. A couple of hours of rest would be good for him. Me too.

He drove into the first gas station we spotted and parked beside the pumps.

Before he could stop me, I was out in a flash and had inserted my credit card into the reader. "Ha-ha. Beat ya."

"You don't have to pay for everything, you know."

"You paid for the rental." Which couldn't have been cheap.

"Need I remind you, I invited you to join me, therefore, I will incur all the associated expenses?"

"Money doesn't grow on trees." Even if he did have a

job that likely paid ten times what I made at the diner, he didn't need to pay for everything. I didn't feel the need to be indebted to him and repay the associated costs.

"Well, thank you. But this is the last thing you'll pay for, understand?"

I nodded, but wholeheartedly disagreed.

He leaned casually against the back of the car and stared off into the distance. It was worthy of a magazine cover image, and I burnt the casual yet somehow sexy image to my brain. Gosh, he had changed so much.

A distraction was needed, at least on my end. "Wow, there's a lot of smoke in the air. All forest fires?"

The air had a bit of a haze to it, but there was a definite campfire type of smell.

"Would be my guess, and likely the number one reason we were grounded."

"You didn't ask?"

"No need. We were going to be parked, and I didn't feel like I was owed an explanation beyond the whole *we'll put you on the next available flight* debacle. I just wanted to get moving, and waiting was going to cost me more than necessary."

His chipper mood was descending, likely due to exhaustion, which was settling hard into the depths of my bones.

I watched the price of the fuel climb higher, and rather

than stare and wait to see the final number, I scanned the area.

As the sun crested the mountain peaks, the smokey skies cast an orangish hue over the sprawling town nestled into the valley below. Another car pulled beside us, and the driver covered his mouth to block out the smoke smell. It wasn't that bad, better than the hot, smoggy days back home.

Holden leaned against the back door of the car, interrupting my thoughts. "What do you want for breakfast, another convenience store dash, or something a little more nutritious? Better yet, what are our options?"

With my eagle eye, I glanced around, searching for possibilities. Fast food joints were in ample supply, and I pointed to one beside a motel. "I know it's not the best, but it'll be quick, and likely more filling than gas station pickings, and cheaper too."

"It's a road trip. Healthy isn't on the menu. It's part of the experience to eat while driving."

My gaze flittered to the motel, thoughts swirling in my head. Ninety percent involved a shower and a place to stretch out, and the other ten were the reason for the shower. It could've been because I was so sleep deprived, but I was seeing Holden in a brand-new ray of sunlight, even if it was somewhat smokey and cast in an orangish glow.

"Do you think they rent out rooms by the hour?"

Holden snapped his head so quick, I worried he'd dislocated his neck. "What?"

"For sleeping, silly." I nudged him playfully. "I'd be willing to bet a breakfast you'd get a better rest on that bed than curled up in a tiny car on the side of the road."

"Uh, maybe." He righted himself and crossed his arms over his chest, a faint tinge of colour on the apples of his cheeks. "But I think it's ridiculous to stay in a room for a few hours."

Still, I allowed the thought to dangle like a carrot as I wanted to make him ponder it as well. "How much further to Victoria?"

He tapped his chin as inhaled sharply. "If we were to drive straight from here..." His fingers swiped across the display on his phone. "At least eight hours to Vancouver."

"Still?" Oh my god, this was going to take way longer than I anticipated. "Eight hours from now puts you there for around four, assuming we don't stop. But... if you rest for a few hours, you can still be in Vancouver just after supper."

"Plus, you're forgetting a ferry ride over to Grandma's house."

"And that." I put the gas pump back into its spot when it clicked off and tore off the receipt, trying my best to keep my eyes from bugging out at the cost.

Holden slid back into the driver's seat and yawned. "Let's get breakfast. Maybe another coffee would help clear my head and make a better plan."

* * *

The smell of a greasy breakfast in the tight space of the car was surprisingly heavenly. I enjoyed the egg and bacon sandwich and the salty crunch of a hashbrown. The coffee needed more sweetening, but it was palatable at least, and I looked forward to the caffeine rush. If Holden was staying awake, it was only fair that I should too. Or at least give it my best effort.

"I'm going to need the ladies' room before we go. Can you park by that store?"

I pointed to another convenience store we passed on the way in. Beside it was a worn-down motel. I'd be foolish to not check on room availability. Surely, we could crash for a couple of hours. For safety, we owed it to ourselves.

We chowed down on our surprisingly filling breakfast in the parking lot.

"Let me go toss the garbage and go to the bathroom while you call your grandparents." I tapped the clock on the dashboard for good measure.

Garbage in hand, I dropped it into the receptacle and peeked quickly at Holden, before I dashed into the main entrance of the rundown motel.

Old fashioned wouldn't even begin to describe the interior. Ancient industrial carpet from the 1950s was wall to wall, and the check-in counter looked like a basement bar set, the kind from the 1970s with the padded front. Hopefully the rooms were in better condition, or at least the bed was reasonably comfortable.

"Can I help you?"

I leaned on the counter and gave my weariest smile. "I sure hope so. My friend and I have been travelling cross country for hours without any rest, and we're flat out exhausted. There's no way we'll make it through the mountain pass without a couple of hours of sleep." I yawned, which added to my plea. "I'm hoping you have a room I can rent for a couple of hours. Nothing fancy, just a clean place to crash, so we don't drive off the side of a mountain by accident."

She gave me a hard stare and cocked an unruly brow which was a complete flip from her perfectly styled hair and expertly applied makeup. "We don't rent rooms by the hour."

That was all she heard. Damn. Needed a change in direction.

"Please. I desperately need a bathroom that isn't an outhouse on the side of the road, where I can wash my hands *with soap*, and I need to stretch my legs." I was grasping at a rapidly fraying rope. "Please. Just for a couple of hours. You can even put me in a recently vacated room as long as one bed is still made up. Surely there must be one of those the cleaning staff haven't yet attended to."

Gross? Absolutely. But sadly, I'd encountered worse. We just need a couple of hours and sleeping in a car didn't provide the best sleep, as I could attest to.

I reached across the counter and used my sweetest voice. "Please. I don't need any amenities, aside from the basics. I can pay cash too, help keep it off the books, if you will? My friend hasn't slept in thirty-six hours, and I swear he's going to nod off soon. I'm terrified we're going to be a mountain-side casualty if he doesn't get any sleep." I glanced at her nametag. "Cindy, please. I'm begging here."

She lowered her voice. "My uncle got an impaired for being so tired."

"That's rough." I mirrored her soft voice. "You understand my pleas, right?"

Nodding her head as her gaze darted around, she typed on the computer. "I'll see what I can find." Her fingers typed rapidly, and once again she searched the area. We were alone. "I have a room, *an untouched room*, on the main floor. I won't give you a code to the pool though."

"That's completely fair. My only plans are for sleeping, not swimming."

Another scan of the lobby. Head down, her fingers clicked faster, and she leaned toward me. "Are you an AMA member?"

I shook my head, not even sure what that was.

She winked and typed extra fast, raising her voice. "I thought you were. With your AMA discount, the best rate I can give you is fifty percent off the regular rack rate but it's a

79

full night's cost."

"How much is that?" I swallowed. My meager savings weren't going to last long between the gas and the food and now a motel cost.

Thankfully, the quote was less than what I had expected to pay for a couple of hours. Even if we only slept for a few hours, it was money well spent.

"I'll take it, thank you, Cindy. You're a life saver." I beamed and put my hands over my heart.

A few minutes later, I walked outside flashing my key.

Holden hung up and met me halfway.

"A rest on a clean mattress beckons you. Two hours, three tops. You'll feel so much better. As will I, and therefore I'll be able to keep you talking all the way to grandma's house. I need you to rest that big brain of yours because I want all the facts as we head west."

He sighed and covered his yawn.

"I know it will delay things a touch, but we can drive straight on through. Only minor gas and food stops."

"Guess I can't say no."

"You could, but it wouldn't be very nice. I had to do some serious sweet-talking in there." There was an unexpected spring in my step. "What do you think? It's only a couple of hours. A nap, not a full out sleep."

"Well, then. I say, thank you. I appreciate this. Let me lock the car."

"Can I grab my bag first?" I intended to freshen up after a quick snooze.

We grabbed our personal effects and walked to the door at the end of the wing. Unlocking it, I stepped inside the tiny space bathed in the 1970s décor I'd completely expected. My foster bedroom had been bigger, but it wasn't the size of the space that made the breath catch in my throat. It was the lonely bed, barely big enough for two people.

"Well, shit."

Chapter Eight

My bag fell from my hand and hit the floor with a thud. I swallowed. "Well, I guess I should've stated we need two beds."

Neither of us moved, we just stared at the barely bigger than twin-sized bed.

"Did you call your grandparents?"

He stared and blinked. "What? Oh, yeah. They're upset but there's nothing they can do. Grandma asked me to give her updates as I stop."

"Oh." Suddenly I was fixated on the *I* part. "Does she know you have a navigator or a travel companion?"

He stepped away from my question, walking to the back of the room to peek inside the bathroom. "It's pretty bare bones, but there's toilet paper, soap, and a fresh set of towels."

I didn't understand where my sudden flare up came from, and I tried my best to keep the pitch out of my tone.

"You told her you were travelling alone?"

He sighed and slumped onto the bed. It bounced and creaked with his movement. "You wouldn't understand."

My arms crossed tightly over my chest, tipping my head to the side. "I might. Try me."

He ran his fingers through his hair and stretched out, giving the bed a little bounce, while totally ignoring my comment. "It's not horrible. Not a cloud or anything, but it'll work."

The fire inside of me burned hotter. "You know, if it's one thing I can't stand, it's being someone's dirty little secret."

I grabbed my bag off the floor and stomped outside, slamming the door behind me. Surely there was a bus depot or something that could get me out of this place. It had been a bad idea to share a road trip with him, especially since he wouldn't admit he had company to his grandparents.

"Iris, wait."

I huffed along, my hair bun bouncing to my stern steps as my flats hit the sidewalk with force.

His hand wrapped around mine. "What in hell is going on? What do you mean, dirty little secret? I never called you that."

Avoiding his gaze, I instead focused on my shoes. "I need my things, please."

"Where will you go?"

I shrugged. "I don't know. But I can't…" A deep ache

was building. Part of the reason I was running away from home was because of secrets. "I hate sneaking around."

"Who's sneaking?" His brows formed a deep V, and he kept a tight focus on me.

"You."

"Because I didn't tell my grandparents?" He pulled a hand over his face and then pinched the bridge of his nose.

I nodded, and my vision blurred. "I can't stand secrets."

"Come on." Holden reached for my hand and lowered his voice. "Let's go back to the room and talk. Tell me what's really bothering you. Besides, we have an audience."

Glancing around, the curtains slammed shut as I glared at the nosy couple staring out their window.

"Come on." He didn't let go of my hand as he guided me back to the room. Once inside, he closed and locked the door. "What's going on?"

"I hate secrecy, and it bothers me that you didn't admit to them how I am in this with you."

"I didn't think it was that big a deal. I'm sorry." The bed made a nasty squeak when he sat, and a hollow echo when he patted the spot beside him. "Tell me why that made you cry?"

My fingers wiped away the tears, and the bed bounced as I fell into beside him. "I left Toronto because of secrets."

"Oh?"

The ache was spreading, the pain still raw and fresh. My hand covered my chest, and my breath came in raspy inhales.

84

Everything was hurting, splitting wide open. The scars hadn't had a chance to fully heal yet.

"My ex, well, he kept secrets. Many of them. I thought I knew him, I thought I knew my friends, but I was just naïve, stupid, or foolish." A deep breath expanded my chest, but I kept my focus on the floor, staring at the circular patterns. "He cheated on me. The whole time we were together."

"Wow. I'm sorry." He was quiet and apologetic, but he didn't move away like I was diseased.

"The worst part is my friends knew it too. All of them. Every. Single. One. No one bothered to tell me, or send me a text or an email, nothing. They were part of the secret, and I only happened to find out by mistake when he was caught red-handed."

That mental image burned brightly in my head. Naked. Together. On his couch.

Now that the words had started rolling, and the proverbial dam busted, I continued with my story. "He made me believe I was special, and repeatedly told me how much he loved and worshipped me. He asked me to move in." Which I'd eagerly accepted so I didn't need to live in my car. "He worked long hours and was often away, and in my stupidity, didn't think anything of it. I thought we were in love. My shifts at the café were sporadic, so when I got off work early, I came home, planning to make him a nice supper, and well, you can figure out the rest."

"Jesus, I'm so sorry." Holden squeezed my hand.

"When I told the person who I thought was my best friend, she admitted she already knew and had little to offer in the way of sympathy. In fact, she said she was surprised I didn't already know. How's that for a kick to the gut?" I dared to look at Holden, who had a serious expression shadowing his features. "Once again, I had no place to live, and no friends to confide in. I had nothing."

"And that's how you wound up at the airport?"

"No. Not entirely." But I wasn't ready to open that door. I'd said enough. More than enough.

"I'm sorry. I had no idea."

"How could you?"

He tenderly held my hand, his thumb tenderly rubbing my knuckles. "Please don't go. Stay with me. Let me make sure you get to the airport in Victoria."

He was so sincere, and his words were like butter.

I smashed my hands against my face and buried into it. "Maybe I'm just tired and because of that, I'm over sensitive about you not telling your grandparents."

"Maybe. Why don't you lay down? That's why you got the room, right?"

I looked at the crisp, white pillow. It appeared fluffy and comfortable.

"Actually, I got this for you. Are you going to sleep?"

"Are we both sleeping on one bed?"

My options were limited. "Tell you what, you sleep and stretch out, and when we're back in the car, I can crash for a bit."

"Nonsense. We're both grown adults. We'll sleep back-to-back if that would make you more comfortable. Do you trust me?"

For some reason, deep down I knew he wouldn't murder me, or worse – take advantage – while I slept. Slowly, I nodded an affirmative, and crawled under the blanket to put a barrier between us as I curled into the pillow, keeping my back to the middle of the bed. He did the same and before he'd stopped shifting around, Mr. Sandman had pulled me under.

* * *

The best dream comforted me like the velvety blankets in the cheap motel room. Holden had snuggled against me, my back toasty warm, his arm draped over my stomach. His deep breathing was rhythmic and steady.

I blinked and smiled.

And slowly came to.

It was no dream. Holden has his arm around me, and my fingers were laced through his. What the hell?

"Holden, get up." I unlinked our hands and reached for my phone. My eyes bugged out when I saw the time. I gave him a shake. "Holy shit! Wake up."

So much for a quick little nap. We'd managed to sleep for five hours straight. The morning had disappeared into early afternoon. Getting into Victoria before midnight was going to be impossible.

"What?" His voice was raw with sleep. "What time is it?"

"It's after two."

"Seriously?" Like he'd been struck by lightning, he leapt off the bed. "Can you be ready to go in ten?"

I shot up, tossing the covers into a messy pile, and rubbed my face. "I'll only need five."

A flurry of activity swirled through the room, and after a quick freshening, Holden grabbed the car while I dropped off the room key, thanking Cindy once more.

I slipped into the passenger seat and opened the maps app. "Barring only a quick ten minute refueling and food grab in, ah... Kamloops, we should be able to make it to the Vancouver ferry terminal in eight hours." I changed the end destination to see what our other option was. "Or ten minutes less, if you park at the airport and fly over to the island."

"I'll need time to think about which way is more practical." He put the car in gear and after a quick lunch grab from another fast-food restaurant, we were racing down the highway – the speed a little north of the limit.

"Have you been through the mountains before?" I asked as the vehicle wove and wound its way around the mountain.

The area was so pretty, and I couldn't stop myself from the passenger seat sightseeing expedition. Trees grew out the sides of the rock, somehow, and in the distance, far below, a river snaked its way between the mountains in the valley. Despite the overcast skies with a hint of dark clouds hanging in the westward direction, the entire view was marvelous. No wonder they'd called that one town Golden. It truly was magnificent.

"Oh yeah, several times. Last time was a couple of years ago, but we only drove from Victoria to Revelstoke. Haven't been this far east in a few years." He removed his gaze from the road for a fraction of a second to glance in my direction. "Have you?"

"Never. Lived in Toronto all my life."

Even though my homes changed every few months, it was always in the Greater Toronto area. It was all I knew.

"Well, if you see anything interesting you'd like to stop at, let me know. A quick leg stretch will never be turned down."

As much as I'd love to stop and see it all, I couldn't do that and hold him back further. As it was, he was going to be super late getting to his grandparents because of me. "I'm just enjoying the view. It's so different than the GTA."

"We can stop."

"Really?"

"Why do you act so surprised?" Holden's brows knit

together in a flash.

"I don't know. Just figured there wasn't a lot of time for sightseeing."

"I'm not saying we'd spend the night or anything, but a quick ten-minute visit a few times isn't out of line. Besides, when will you be back this way?"

I shook my head. My future was unwritten, but very likely didn't include any more cross-country travels. "No idea."

He laughed, and one-handed the steering wheel as he took another swig of coffee. "Are you a live every moment as it comes, or do you live life more reactionarily?"

I huffed and twisted in my seat. "I'm not sure. I haven't always had the easiest life."

"Although I'm not sure I can say the same about my own childhood, I can empathize. Being grades ahead of your classmates isn't always easy."

"I guess not." I twiddled my thumbs, trying to stop myself from staring as his lips curled around the lid of the coffee cup. "How old were you when you started advancing?"

He gave his chin a thoughtful rub. "Grade two? My teacher was amazing and told my parents I was reading and learning at least two grade levels ahead. For what should've been my grade three year was part grade four and part grade five."

"And you didn't find it hard?"

He shook his head, and a teasing smile stretched across his full lips. "I'd finally felt like I wasn't bored. The classes were more enjoyable, and I easily caught on to whatever was being taught. I started middle school at nine."

"Nine? Wow." Most middle schoolers started when they were eleven, going on twelve, or close to it. Definitely not at nine. "So, you're really smart then."

He shrugged. "Maybe. But I don't like to make a big deal out of it."

"Modest too." I smirked and stared at an outcropping with a tiny waterfall trinkling from a small hole. "How did you fall into rocketry?"

"Through a computer game called Kerbal. Ever play?"

I shook my head. "Games aren't my style."

Nor were computers if I were being honest. They were great until they acted up, which mine did regularly. I was ninety-five percent sure my ancient laptop had a foot in the grave and wouldn't start up when I got to my new destination.

Holden continued. "I loved building the rockets and flying the Kerbans, those are the little aliens, into space. You need to understand a lot of flight dynamics and velocities, and it was right up my alley. After my homework was all completed, I played Kerbal until bedtime."

"Obsessed much?"

"I really loved it and the mechanics behind it, so I started taking online college level courses while still in grade eleven.

91

The teachers at St. Jude's were really good to me, and very encouraging. They pushed me hard, especially when I told them about the courses. The students sucked of course, aside from my best friend, Jeremy."

Right. The huge football star in the NFL.

"By the way, I don't recall seeing you around in grade eleven." Holden tipped his head and raised both his brows in question.

"Yeah, I got a new home."

"You moved around a lot?"

I turned away and watched as another sign warning for falling rocks passed by. "All part of being the badass foster child. House to house."

"Jesus. That's hard to imagine."

"It's hard to live."

"Have you always been a foster child?"

Inhaling sharply, I studied his face for sincerity. It's not like I kept that part of my life under wraps, but it was still not usually something I discussed. "My mom abandoned my dad and I when I was two or maybe three? Just up and left one day. Dad never handled the abandonment well and decided raising a kid on an overnight stock clerk salary wasn't what he wanted to do with his life, so one night when I was five, he didn't come home."

"At all?"

I shrugged. "Nope. I wandered over to the neighbours at

some point, but he never came home, and they called the cops. After that, I got a new home. But it changed frequently. Nothing longer than a year, eighteen months if I was lucky." And that was the longest stint in one place. "Most averaged weeks at best."

Holden went tight-lipped and shoved his fingers through his hair. "Was adoption an option?"

"I honestly don't know. I was a kid. Maybe. But maybe they chose not to add me permanently to their families, for whatever reason. Wow, would you look at that?" I pointed to a monument as we passed by. "We're at the highest point in the Rocky Mountains."

From my left, Holden released a breath. "Well, not really, no. Technically, we're only at the highest place on this highway. There are mountain peaks that are higher, the tallest of which is Mount Robson in Jasper National Park, quite north of here."

"Whatever. Still, it's pretty cool."

Holden pulled into the rest stop at Roger's Pass, and we took a quick tour of the wooden arch monument. However, it was freezing cold, even in August, so we took a few pictures, and hopped back into the warmth of the rental car.

I sat back in my seat and stared at the tops of the mountains, with their snow-white caps as Holden continued to journey westward.

The clouds had parted for a second, and a ray of

sunshine gave a diamond-encrusted glitter to the top of one. I enjoyed my view, thankful I wasn't the one with a deep-seated focus on the road, like Holden. However, he was a source of wild and random facts as we travelled further west, through another town, and then over a river.

Signs with names like *Crazy Creek* whipped by on my right as we sped a whole two kilometers over the speed limit along the two-lane highway. At this pace, our arrival time in Vancouver would get later and later. Since he had left Golden in a rush, I figured we'd stay that way, but somewhere along the highway, his speed dropped to the limit.

"Boy oh boy. I'm going to have two come back and visit these places – they have such fascinating names. Does BC seriously have a place called the Enchanted Forest? What makes it so magical?" Figured he'd be able to spout all sorts of random trivia, and if it kept him talking, it kept him awake. I had noticed a yawn or two from him not long after leaving Roger's Pass.

"It's a touristy place for families. I used to visit with my family on the way to Grandma's house."

"Ah, a tourist trap. Gotcha." Those were a dime a dozen back in Toronto, and most weren't anything to rave about.

"Do you want to stop, and check it out?" There was such hope in his voice.

"No way. I've already cost you time on this trip with my brilliant idea for a two-hour rest that turned into five. We need to get you to Victoria. You have big plans."

"That'll still happen, but if I'm going to be late, what's another couple of hours?" He kept his eyes focused on the road as he pulled around a curve. "What do you say? Do you want to check it out?"

There was so much excitement in his voice, it was hard to turn down. Although I had all the time in the world, at least now I did, Holden didn't. However, the offering of a stop and a stretch of the legs would be welcome. It had been an hour since we our last stop.

"Sure, why not? As long as you don't hold it against me."

He gave me a quizzical look. "Wouldn't dream of it."

"Then let's do it. Show me this Enchanted Forest."

Chapter Nine

The vehicle slowed as he signaled and pulled into a parking lot flanked on either side by blue pointy buildings.

Tucked along the edge of the parking lot were small versions of castles, fairytale creatures, and quaint little cottages, as if brought to life from a children's storybook and dropped into the forest.

"This will be great." Like a child on Christmas morning, he was lit up from the inside out, and it thrilled me to see this side of him. "You'll see."

I tipped my head and followed him to the ticket booth. "If you say so."

"It's a quick tour. Think it takes less than an hour to see the whole thing, even if you're lollygagging. At least it did when I was little."

The Enchanted Forest certainly lived up to its name. After we paid, the hum from the highway died away as we stepped deeper into the thick, densely packed forest. The smell of earth and trees and nature surrounded us, calming me with each inhale. It was a far cry from the urban scents of a downtown metropolis.

"I used to love coming here as a child." The megawatt smile on his face never faded. "My parents would have my sister and I hunt for the fairies, and we'd hang out in the world's tallest treehouse thinking we were the greatest people ever. It was fun pretending we were ethereal."

I didn't know what that meant, although I assumed it was positive, but I mocked it with a teasing grin regardless. "Today's word of the day is *ethereal*."

He returned the comment with a playful bump against my shoulder.

"Tell me more about this treehouse."

The cool kids on sitcoms, with their perfectly involved parents, always had treehouses, and they were always built together over a weekend of smiles. I didn't think they were anything more than something created for tv. However, if there was a real treehouse here, I wasn't leaving until I saw it in person.

"I'll show you." Without hesitation, he reached for my hand and tugged me along.

I would've let go or shook myself free from his warmth, but deep down I was enjoying the connection just a little too much. I hadn't had a genuine touch like that in ages.

Along the packed dirt paths, between little villages of cartoon characters, most of which were as unfamiliar to me as rocket science, Holden led the way. He delighted in mentioning all their names and when I often got a perplexed expression, told me which cartoons they came from. Which helped. A little. I clearly hadn't watched as much tv as he had.

"What was your favourite fairytale?" He paused under a cow jumping over a thin crescent of a moon. Shoulders relaxed, he rested his weight on one foot, an innocent, youthful joy making him look even younger than he was.

"I don't really know a lot of these stories."

"No one ever read fairytales to you?" His eyes widened in mock horror, although maybe he was really concerned.

I shook my head and glanced around, spying gnomes or dwarfs, and a variety of colourful characters. "No one had the time when I was little, and as I grew up, other reads were more attractive."

"I'm so sorry."

"Because we had different childhoods?"

It was just the way things were. Foster homes weren't known for being excellent, nurturing homes, at least not the ones I was forced to be a part of.

I shrugged and walked ahead, kicking a pebble out of the way. "What was your favourite fairytale?"

"Peter Pan," he said without skipping a beat. No delay, no hesitation.

"What was so exciting about Peter Pan?"

"What wasn't?" His voice pitched in excitement. "He had no responsibilities, no curfews, and lived the life he wanted under his own terms. He got to enjoy being a kid, with endless adventures, and no matter what happened, he always managed to defeat the evil Captain Hook." He mimed having a sword and jumped forward to pretend to stab something or someone. "It's the greatest story ever told."

"Really? Would you say you're more like Peter Pan or one of the Lost Boys?" I only knew of the story through a tv show that twisted fairytales into modern day stories, so I wasn't sure how accurate it was. Pan, as he was called, was an evil little shit, and I was constantly rooting for the charming, and good-looking, Hook.

He gave his chin a scratch and victorious in his imaginary battle, sat on a toadstool. "Hmmm… I'd say more like one of the Lost Boys, but not really. Maybe more like Peter in the fact that I'll never find true love."

Except he was looking right at me, and a faint rush of heat blanketed my body as my blood pulsed double time. "Oh, I'm sure you'll find it one day."

"Even if Wendy did like me, it'll never happen. I can never get off the island. I'm forever trapped." Scrubbing his face, he pulled himself to a stand and wandered away.

As he'd spoken, his face morphed from childlike joy into one of a heavy-handed seriousness, and his footsteps slowed with the deep weight of darkened secrets you can't let the light shine upon. And I would know, I had a master's degree in keeping secrets locked away.

But it opened the door to many questions I had but wouldn't dare give breath too. It wasn't my place to vocalize, as I wouldn't want him poking and prodding into my life in return, however, I was curious about the island. We were headed to Vancouver Island – is that what he meant? Once he was there, he was trapped? Or did he mean it metaphorically? Like he was stuck in his life, which didn't seem correct as he had everything he wanted and had planned for.

I gave my head a quick shake and caught up when he stopped a few feet away. Behind him was a giant treehouse. The biggest one in BC, according to the sign. And it was unlike anything I'd ever seen on tv or imagined.

"See?" A self-satisfied tone ribboned through the word, almost like an ah-hah. "Want to check it out?"

We stood at the base of the first set of stairs, beside artfully placed rocks, and bright, red-topped giant mushrooms. The first house we had to walk through on our ascent was only a dozen or so stairs above the path. After that, another narrower flight of steps curved around the tree, climbing to the second house. From there, a final set twisted higher to the third and topmost house, perched halfway up the impressively tall pine tree.

"Sure. Nothing like a little adventure." Or a workout.

By the time we ascended to the tiny, and empty room, at the top I was hot, and my sweatshirt stuck to parts of my back. How very unattractive. Absentmindedly, I pushed up the sleeves, exposing my arms. When I caught sight of Holden's stare, I quickly dropped them down again.

"Can I ask?" His eyes stayed glued on my arms. "Twenty Questions style?"

My life experiences weren't a game, but I understood his weak desire to ask. It seemed less threatening, although he wasn't playing the game correctly. I looked up the rules a couple of hours ago. They were all supposed to be leading to one answer.

Oh. I hesitated with that realization. The one answer was why – why had I tried to take my own life? "Maybe, but note I may not answer."

It was a gentle nod of affirmation, but he agreed.

"What do you want to know?" I leaned my butt against the railing and admired the view of greenery off the side of the hut. Some of the trees were leafy varieties but most were Christmas type ones, and I bet it smelled great over the holidays.

"One. Did it hurt?" He reached for my hand and gently turned it over, pushing the sleeve up and exposing my inner arm. Ever so gently, he avoided the thickest scab and ran his thumb over one of the faded yet raised scars.

Although I wasn't cold, I still shivered at the tender

touch. "No more than the loneliness."

His other hand cradled my arm, and he trailed a soft finger down from the scar into the palm of my hand, making two little circles. "I'm so sorry. Loneliness is a bitch."

"At least you have your family." It came out with the wrong tone and even worse inflections, and immediately I felt awful for having opened my mouth. "I'm sorry. I didn't mean it like that."

"No, it's okay. I understand. And you're right, I do have family. I can't even begin to imagine what it's like to not have my sister around, as much of a pain in the ass that she is." He laughed, and the sound of it settled my electrified nerves.

"Did I ever know her?"

"No. Myriam went to an all-girls school, since well…" He looked me in the eyes but didn't break the hold he had with my hand. "I became an uncle at fourteen."

My eyes widened. "How much age difference is there between you?"

"She's two years older."

My age. As careless as I was at that age, I always doubled-bagged. Becoming a mother at sixteen was not in my cards. "Oh, wow."

"I've never met my nephew. He was adopted by a family in Quebec, a good family we were told, one that promised to love and care for him."

Oh god, had my foster home woes worried him?

"I'm sure if he was adopted, then he was very much wanted and will be well taken care of." I held his hand. "Did he have a name?"

"Not that we heard. He was Baby deLauer when Myriam handed him off, pretty much sight unseen. She pushed him out and they took him away. He'd be nine now." A veil of sadness covered him like the clouds over the sun. A haunted, far-off expression ghosted across his eyes.

If it was one thing I could do well, it was read the room, and a change in topic was definitely requested. "You know, if he's anything like you, he'd probably love it here. This place really is enchanted."

"That it is." He stood impossibly close, enough to smell a hint of peppermint from the piece of gum he was chewing.

My eyes roamed over his tanned cheeks and focused on his lips. His perfectly formed lips. They appeared soft and touchable, and just thinking about it increased the tempo of my heart.

"Fairytales are amazing. Even though you know the hero will defeat the villain by the end of the story, the journey is worth watching. The characters all get what they want, and there's a guaranteed happy ending. But real life isn't a fairytale, and I'm no hero. There's so much I want but can't have." He ran his hand up my arm and looped it around my waist, gently tugging me close – the air between us full of sparks.

I swallowed, my heart thumping against my ribs. "You're working hard to achieve everything you want, and no doubt, you'll get it all."

"No, not everything."

We stood so close the breeze couldn't channel its way through.

"Do you believe in happy endings?" His words were low and throaty, and the vibrations of it stirred up a longing deep inside.

"Is that your second question?" I laughed, but his face was all seriousness. "Oh, we're not playing anymore?" I looked deep into his eyes. "I don't know if I believe."

Breathlessly, I moved my head closer and stared into the depths of his eyes; they matched the mossy greenery of the forest. My heart pounded and my hands tingled. I wanted so much to give into the urge to lean forward and plant a teasing kiss on him, and as much as I believed that was what he wanted, I held back.

"Iris?" The whisper of my name tickled the strings in my heart.

"Holden?"

We gazed at the other, barely a wisp of breath between us. Slowly, with a hint of hesitation, he tipped toward me and ever so parted his lips. Before we sealed together, he pulled back and stared.

"I really shouldn't."

"You can, it's okay." Unable to stop myself, I took the lead and brushed my lips over his, my legs weakening a touch the moment we connected.

He was an inexperienced kisser, stiff and a little sloppy, but after few heartbeats, the kiss changed in power, and the throbbing sensations it produced turned my legs to jelly and sent my pulse racing into outer space.

"I shouldn't have done that." His voice fell. "I'm sorry."

Of course, there was instant regret on his part. It was me, after all – a former bully who was only as smart as a stick. Turning away, with white knuckle ferocity my hands curled around the railing as I lowered my heavy embarrassment between my arms.

He placed his hands on my shoulders and tenderly ran them down to rest above mine.

I had the uncanny ability to detach myself from most people, to not get caught up in emotions, except once, and after that explosion, I swore to myself it would never happen again. I simply was not the kind of person someone as kind and wholesome as Holden should ever be caught up in. I was a raging disaster, and his post-kiss apology was proof of that.

"We should get going. Your family is waiting." I dropped out from under him and descended the tower of stairs, my feet smacking the steps in a fury to leave.

Holden kept pace and soon we were at the entrance which, coincidentally, had us walk through the gift shop.

"Before we go, I need a memento. For the memories."

Since we were on his schedule, I waited patiently as he searched through the racks of tacky tourist traps, until he settled on a snow globe of all things. Inside were miniature gnomes sitting on toadstools, the words *Enchanted Forest* on a sign behind the shortest gnome, as glitter floated all around the dome.

"Do you always grab a tacky souvenir from your stops?"

"Every single time."

I snorted and put my hand on my hip. "You didn't grab one at the airport, or at the motel."

"Who says I didn't?" He wiggled his eyebrows. "Not every souvenir needs to be a tacky one."

My eyes widened, since I was the one who had a dark past. "What did you take?"

"I didn't steal anything, if that's what you're thinking." He nudged me, and I was relieved to see that sweet smile on his face again. "But I did find this rock behind the car at the motel when I loaded the suitcases."

From the pocket of his jeans, he retrieved a spotted rock with amber-coloured streaks. It was unlike anything I'd seen before.

"Wow, that's really pretty."

He dropped it into my hand, the weight of it surprised me. "I'm a bit of a rock collector, perhaps a tiny little geologist lives in me. Corny, right?"

I shook my head, thinking how unique it was and wondering how big his rock collection had to be. "Not at all."

We walked out to the rental car, and Holden remotely unlocked it.

"Can you help me find a rock?" I tipped my head to the side and thrust my hands into my pockets.

He bridged the gap between us. "Seriously?"

"Why not? I happen to think it's a cool tradition. Since I'm starting my life over, now is as good a time as any to pick up a new tradition too. Is there a method to how you choose?" I spotted an outcropping of rocks around a tree trunk and with a spring in my step headed over.

Searching high and low I stumbled across one that fit our impromptu stop perfectly. It was a rounded triangle, like a gnome's hat, in a faint greyish orange hue. "Does this work? Orange is my favourite colour."

"It's perfect." Holden scooped his own off the ground and lifted the speckled rock up to admire. Without a word, he pocketed it and extended his hand. "Off to Vancouver we go, but first, I'll call Grandma and update her."

It was probably a smart idea to text Amber and do the same. At least with her, the text would be quick.

Holden held open the door while I hopped in. "Hey, Grandma." He carefully closed it and walked around the car, sliding into his space. "Just leaving the Enchanted Forest... Yes, I'm aware how far I still have to go... Yes, I'm know I'm expected to be in tip-top shape on Monday morning at the university, after my night at the observatory." He rolled his eyes.

At least she cares.

A weary sigh breathed out and he looked my way. "Best guess? Probably not until after midnight. Maybe later... No, don't wait up... Well, first I need to find out if I fly over or take the ferry. Haven't figured that out yet... Yes, as soon as I know, you'll know... Love you too."

I turned and focused on the blue entrance markers a few feet away, trying in earnest to keep my thoughts from turning selfish.

I wasn't good enough for him, and the fact of the matter was he knew it too. He pulled back after the kiss, apologized and said it shouldn't have happened. Even if he got swept away in the moment, since I had been the one to initiate it, maybe he remembered who I was – a homeless, high-school dropout. How could I ever compete with him? He was so smart, he leveled up easily in both school and university, and now has a prestigious job waiting for him at the crack of dawn in something like thirty-six hours. How did someone like me even compete with that?

I couldn't.

That's why he apologized.

Chapter Ten

I had to make the best of a tough situation. Regardless of my growing feelings for Holden, it would never happen. We were too different to make it work. Rather than make misery for the remainder of our road trip, I set my feelings aside. For my sanity, I had too. Dissociation was my middle name.

"We're about an hour outside of Kamloops." I tossed a gaze over to the gas tank. "Think we'll make it that far?"

Holden stared at it before flipping his attention back to the road, his lips mumbling as he performed some calculations in his head. "We've gone 260 on this tank, and roughly another 100 to go, and we've used just over half the tank which is always bigger… Yeah, I think we'll make it. It'll be tight but provided we don't have to slow down for traffic snarls, we should be good."

"Should we stop outside of Kamloops?"

"Nah, the gas'll be more expensive than in the major centre. We'll keep going. If I think it's getting dangerously low, then I'll stop quickly and pump in five or ten bucks to keep us going."

He dug around behind my seat.

"What are you looking for?"

"My bag of treats."

"From this morning's convenience grab and go?"

"You make it sound like we stole things." He winked. "But yes, that bag."

"Oh, you finished everything off a while ago, and I'd tossed the bag of garbage at the rest stop back at Roger's Pass."

"Dang, I'm hungry. I need a snack."

I had nothing to offer. My banana and lone chocolate bar were long gone too. "Are you always hungry? Or is this just a road trip thing?"

"I snack a lot on road trips. It's all part of the experience." Holden one handed the steering wheel. "Want to play a game?"

"You love games too, don't you?"

A sly, mischievous grin stretched from ear to ear. "Who doesn't? You don't?"

"No, I do. I've just never played games on the road."

"That's because you've never travelled with me."

I heartily laughed because it was totally true. "Sure,

what's the game?"

"It's a form of the license plate game, except, instead of seeing how many different provinces or states we see, we'll take the first three letters on the plate and make a reverse acronym."

"I don't follow." I twisted in my seat to get a better look at him.

"Like the car ahead, the first three letters are AJG, so you could say *always jog graciously*."

An unexpected laugh burst out of me imagining that. "No one jogs graciously, but it's funny. I like it."

"What do you mean? I jog graciously."

My eyebrow went so high it likely joined my hair line. "Let me guess. Your Apple watch monitors your steps and speed, sending data to you through your ear pods, all the while your breathing is evenly paced with controlled inhales and exhales. Your arms pump just so, and you're light enough on your feet to resemble a gazelle."

Holden didn't speak, however I didn't miss the upward twist of his lips.

"Am I right?"

"Not about the gazelle part."

I couldn't hold back my smile.

Okay, your turn, Miss Smartypants."

"Hmm…" I rubbed my chin. I wasn't good thinking on my feet. "Another jet goof."

"Not bad."

"It sucks." But another thought jumped into my head. "Abrasive jewelry maker."

"Not a good slogan for their company." But there was a twinkle in his eye, and I was thrilled to see it.

We went back and forth on a few, as we weren't passing anyone, and no one was passing us. Finally, a fresh vehicle pulled in front.

"RAF," Holden announced, but before I could throw out a reverse acronym, he continued, "Royal Air Force."

"Too easy." I patted his hand which sat lazily on the arm rest between us. "That already exists. What about? Road trips are fun."

"Yeah. I like that." He pointed to a sign. "I've always wanted to see that place, and I'm hungry. Can we stop?"

"Time is my luxury, not yours."

"Then I'm making the call. We're stopping."

Holden pulled into the turn lane, and drove up the gravel road, parking near a quaint roadside eatery. From the highway, this place would've been missed, if not for the sign. We were high above the highway, and a gorgeous valley stretched out below.

"You grab the table; I'll grab the food. You're not allergic to anything?"

"Not that I've found out."

"Ooh, they serve wine. Want one?" Holden swayed on

his feet with excitement.

But I shook my head. "No, thanks. Just something with caffeine, like a Coke or Pepsi."

I ambled over to one of three vacant picnic tables situated near the edge of the cliff area. Down below, the highway wove around the vineyards stretching out in the valley with the setting sun blanketing the grapevines in golden hues. It was breathtaking and I snapped a picture. I turned and took one of Holden standing at the walk-up window of the eatery.

The weathered and rickety table wobbled as I sat on one side.

"This place is amazing."

Holden waved the tray of steaming food between us as I continued taking in the jaw-dropping view. "It is."

"Thank you." I took a bite of my chicken wrap. It was the first thing I'd eaten since the motel, and until I sunk my teeth into the meaty texture, I didn't know I was so famished. "Let me guess, your parents took you here too?"

"Absolutely not, mom always packed lunches. Take out was a cost they didn't need, but she always managed to find the best places to have a picnic at, so it never felt like we were missing anything." He drifted off with a dreamy expression on his face. Must be nice to look back fondly on your childhood. "However, I've always wanted to come here but never had the chance."

"Until now."

"Until now." He smiled and took a sip from the plastic wine glass of his chardonnay. "You should taste it. It's magnificent."

Like a neon sign, it called out to me, and it was impossibly hard to turn down. I wanted to feel the tingle of the sparkling grapes as they passed over my lips and tickled my tastebuds. But rather than test my crumbling strength, I politely declined. One taste was never enough. "It's part of the reason I can't drive."

"Why's that?" He gave me his full attention.

I inhaled sharply, tore my focus off Holden, and threw it back over to the setting sun.

It wasn't like we were going to be an item, so throwing a little fuel on the fire wasn't going to hurt. "I had a little too much to drink one night, and in my stupid state of mind, I drove home. And I got caught."

"Jesus."

"The details are too gruesome to share, but some claim it wasn't an accident, not really, that I had purposely hit the tree in the ditch."

"Had you?" He leaned forward to take in my every word.

"No. *That* was an accident – totally unplanned – but the moments following it were definitely not, however, I lost my license for thirty days. DUI." My heart raced in anticipation of what I was about to share. "But it gets worse. I was in the darkest point in my life and saw no way out. I'd just lost my job, I'd recently found out my boyfriend was a piece of shit, and my friends weren't much better." Deep, ripping pain seared through my chest, and I stared at the plastic tray between us. "Having survived the crash somehow, I'd spied a shard of glass and took matters into my own hands." I blinked and focused on Holden's bright green eyes.

"Oh?" His Adam's Apple bobbed once as he choked down a swallow.

"Unsuccessfully."

"Jesus, I'm sorry." His jaw slackened and he inhaled and held his breath for a moment. "But is it wrong of me to say I'm glad you were unsuccessful. You're here now." His soft hand covered mine. "You're worth it, you know."

"But I don't."

"You are."

I stared at the base of his wine glass, gnawing desire wrapping its spiraled tentacles around my soul. "I'm a mess of epic proportions. Never had my head on straight, and I'll never amount to anything."

"That's not true. You just don't believe in yourself."

I shrugged. "Hard to believe in myself when everyone tells me I'm worthless, and I have the endless qualifications to back it up. A high school dropout. A homeless piece of trash."

"You're homeless?"

I avoided his sympathetic half-grin. "My car was my home. Until the accident."

"Wow."

"All I literally have is what's in your car." I hung my head.

One suitcase with a few pieces of secondhand clothes and even fewer personal effects. Not even enough to fill a vehicle. That's what my life was worth now.

Stroking my hand from knuckle to fingertip soothed my rapidly fraying nerves. How did he manage to calm me? Was it the gentle touch? The compassion in his eyes?

"Having problems doesn't make you a bad person - it makes you real. Yes, your problems are kind of a big deal, but there are ways of tackling them and setting yourself up for success."

"You sound like a therapist."

He chuckled. "Ah, so you've met one?"

It made a weak smile pop out, and I lifted my hand, splaying my fingers. "Foster home number fourteen. It was part of the deal of going there. Weekly visits with Dr. Brain Picker."

"How long did you go?"

A light breeze swirled, and a shudder washed over me.

"Until my foster mother kicked me out a month later. Teenage girls with high hormones and no moral standards weren't allowed to live in her home."

It was a surprise to no one when I came home from school and saw my social worker at the front door. I gathered the few things I hadn't taken to school, and ten minutes later we were off to another temporary place.

"It is what it is." It wasn't like I could turn back the clock or anything. "I'm really looking forward to staying with my cousin. She travels quite a bit and says it would be me doing her the favour if I stayed at her place and kept it from falling apart. She runs the local pub there." Nothing like facing your demons head on, right? But she had faith in me, more than was warranted, however, I wasn't going to let her down. Or at least, try my best.

"So, you do have family?" A smirk stretched across his lips.

"No, not really. Amber's not a blood relative or anything, at least not to me. Sort of a long story, but she's the cousin of one of the foster families I stayed with. Amber and I chatted and exchanged emails, and eventually, she became a friend. She knew bits and pieces about what was going on in my life and told me her door was always open, even though it was across the country. After a bit of soul searching, right after the accident, I called her up, asked if that offer was still on the table, and here I am on my way to meet her in real life."

"See, you're already sowing the seeds of success. You reached out for help."

"I guess." I picked at the edge of the foil wrapper,

folding it and pressing a firm crease along its length.

"That had to have been incredibly hard."

"Are you sure you're not the therapist? You sound like one." I cocked an eyebrow and picked up my wrap for another bite.

"Then I'd better stop. I get the impression you don't like many medical professionals and I'd hate for you to start disliking me, especially when we're becoming friends." He patted my hand and chased down his wine.

"Is that what we are?" I cocked an eyebrow as I lowered my head. This time I was digging. I wanted more. Was he saying it out of compassion, or because he meant it? I hoped for the second one because, aside from the medical professionals and the cops, I hadn't told a soul what had happened that night. Even Amber didn't have all the details.

"Like I said on the plane, you'll always have a friend in me."

The theme song from a kid's movie played in my head, and I started laughing as I heard the words.

"Was what I said funny?" He pushed himself up to a stand and stretched out his back.

"Not at all. I was just thinking of *Toy Story*." The melody continued to play in my head as I gathered the garbage onto the tray.

Holden stood in front of me, a soft yet warm expression on his face as he took the tray from my hands and set it back on the table. "Thank you."

I stared up at him, a million thoughts racing through my head. "For what?"

"For sharing. It's a tough thing to do, and I'm really glad you opened up to me."

Air whooshed out of my lungs and for a heartbeat I forgot how to breath. Inhaling a steady breath, I focused on his full lips, wondering – hoping – for another moment like we had at the treehouse. "You're welcome."

His gaze danced between my eyes as if he wasn't sure which eye he should focus on as he inched a little closer. His lips parted, just enough.

I was going to let him take the lead; to see if there was something brewing between us or if I'd read too much back at the treehouse.

His phone buzzed. "It's Grandma." He waved it in the air. "I need to take this."

I stared at his back as he walked a few steps away. Rather than dwell on it, I dumped the garbage in the trash and dropped off the tray at the walkup window. "Food was great, thank you."

Holden met me near the little building. "We should get a move on. Still a few hours to Vancouver, and we haven't figured out yet if we'll ferry it over or fly."

"You're okay to drive?" I asked Holden.

A week ago, driving drunk, or even getting into a

vehicle with someone who was intoxicated, wouldn't have been a thought I'd hesitate to entertain, and yet, now there was this desire to… I shook my head, unable to complete the idea. Why did I suddenly care if we were safe or not?

He stopped walking and gave me his full attention. "I promise I'm good to drive. This little bit of wine will not affect me, not with all this food I just ate."

"Okay." The word limped out.

"Iris, I promise, you're safe with me." He stepped closer and unexpectedly, dropped a kiss on my forehead.

It was too intimate, and quite unusual for him to have been so forward, although it warmed my heart with his sweet, casual gesture, like we were truly old friends.

I stepped back, catching my breath. "How about while you drive, I'll look into what's available, flight versus ferry, what the prices are, and all that fun stuff? But I'll need a phone cord. My battery is draining."

"I have one you can use."

"Thanks."

After a quick bathroom break, we walked to the car, and I stole another glance at the valley. I took a variety of pictures.

"What about me?" Holden jumped into the shot.

"The light's hitting your back so you're all in shadow. Turn around." I walked in front and snapped a pic of him with the chicken wrap sign in the background.

"Now together."

We posed side by side, the golden hues of the setting sun casting a warm glow over both of us. He smiled brightly, and I couldn't help but echo his expression. Framing us perfectly, I clicked a few times. My heart beat a little faster, and although I hadn't touched the alcohol, I felt a tad tipsy with his arm around my waist.

"Thank you for that." Regardless of what would happen, I knew I'd treasure that picture always.

Holden snatched a rock from beside his foot. "For what?"

"For letting me join you on this trans-Canada trip. In case I forget to tell you later, I'm having a really good time." Before I had a chance to rescind, I planted a kiss on his cheek.

He turned into it.

For a heartbeat we were sealed together in a knee-weakening embrace.

In the glow of the setting sun.

In the warmth of a Saturday evening on a long weekend.

On a mountain side turnout.

It would've been romantic had it not been so cheesy.

It would've been perfect if Holden hadn't spoken.

"Oh, please don't post our picture on social media."

"Huh?" Stunned wouldn't have been the right word. Gobsmacked summed it up better. "I haven't posted anything about this trip."

"Well, I've seen you on there."

"Yeah, scrolling." Stalking my *friends'* pages, checking my IMs to see if they've inquired as to where I've been. It had just proven my point that it was best to have left it all behind. Good riddance to them all. However, the perfect moment with Holden had been ruined, and sarcasm laced my words. "We're not even connected, so you're good."

"I can change that, you know." He opened an app on his phone to show me.

"I think right now it's more important we get moving." I patted his arm and sent a quick text to Amber, updating her.

She responded quickly how late it would be by the time we arrived in Victoria, but she said she'd get back to me tomorrow morning with a flight out of there. Her pilot friend Eric didn't fly in the evening, and since he was my ride to Cheshire Bay, it depended on which flight had room in his tomorrow's runs. My plans now included another overnight stay. Somewhere.

Once back on the highway, I relayed what Amber had said.

"Grandma said the same thing."

"Is she leaving the house unlocked for you or a key under the mat?"

He kept his focus on the road. "No, but she said she'd stay awake until I arrive."

Calculating the drive ahead, plus whatever ferry or flight we could find, there'd be no way he'd get to the house before two am, and that was being generous.

"It's going to be super late when you finally get there. We shouldn't have stopped. I'm so sorry." Fully prepared to handle the burden, I sunk into my seat.

"I'm not too worried, and you shouldn't be either." He held his breath for a minute before he stole a quick peek in my direction. "Besides… I already told her I'll be grabbing a hotel room, and I'd be home before noon tomorrow."

"You what? A hotel room?" The last three words dangled in the air but when he didn't elaborate, I focused on the big picture of what he'd said. "That's cutting it way too close."

"It only gives me a little visit with them before I start work, that's true." He tapped his finger against his chin. It was playful as if he'd already thought that through.

"Yeah, like half a day."

He laughed. "A little more than that, but I'll have the day with them, and then everything will be all switched."

"How so?"

"I'll have late afternoons at the university, and evenings and nights at the observatory. I won't be home until the sun starts coming up."

"And that's why you wanted to be there for the weekend?"

"Precisely."

"And the unscheduled landing changed all that?"

He reached for my hand and gave it a tender squeeze. "But in a good way. I'm getting to know you – the real you. Plus, I've never done a road trip without family along, and this has been entertaining and interesting."

Interesting was a great word for it.

Still, it gave me pause. Enough to speak about it. "And what happens after we get to our destination?"

He put a finger up to stop me. "No. We're not going there. We're going to live in this moment, right now. This time is for us. Sunday night will be here quick enough, and then I'll have to press play once more. Tonight? Let's enjoy the hell out of it. You with me?"

"You sure the wine hasn't hit you?" I gave him a quizzical look.

"Positive. So many things will change the moment I walk in the door at my grandparent's house, that I don't even want to think about it. I just want to be here with you, on this drive, and having fun."

"I like the sound of that. Living in the moment. I can do that."

Someone once had told me about taking a moment in time to forget about the troubles – maybe it was a shrink? – but it sounded like something I could finally do. Whereas Holden had his whole life planned out, and as he'd stated, his life was just about to have the play button activated. I'd lived on replay for far too long, always playing the same thing over and over, hoping for a different outcome. Maybe all I needed was to press pause on my problems, and have a commercial break, so to speak.

For the first time in forever, there was a sparking of hope flickering to life in my soul. A chance to try something completely different and a choice to be a better me.

What in the hell was happening? This wasn't the Iris I knew. But I liked her.

Chapter Eleven

The sun had long set, and the inky darkness surrounded us when we arrived at the hotel.

After some research, we learned the ferries shut down at dusk and we'd missed our last opportunity hours ago. If we dropped off the car and flew over to Victoria, we'd need a cab to any hotel on the island, and that would be twice the cost of staying on the mainland in Vancouver and keeping the rental to ferry over in the morning. In the end, as these things always do, finances won the battle.

However, thanks to my amazing internet sleuthing, I'd found a smoking deal at a place not far from the ferry terminal, and that's where we ended our Saturday road trip adventure.

Key in hand, and weary from the non-stop drive, we entered the room.

"Are you sure they gave you the right key?" Holden's voice held more surprise than the look upon his face after he flicked on the lights.

The room we received was beyond my wildest dreams; we didn't get the wrong key, we got the wrong price. They had to have missed a number or decimal place. The cost was the same, and came with a free continental breakfast, yet this was easily twice the place in elegance and space as the rinky-dink motel we stayed at for a few hours this morning.

Shit, had it really been only a few hours ago?

"All I'd requested was a comfortable bed, a place to clean up, and maybe something with a view, since I wasn't sure when I was going to be visiting the area again. But hey, at least there's two beds this time."

Two queen-sized beds, complete with fluffy white bedding and more pillows than I could quickly count. I imagined laying on it would be like sleeping on a cloud.

Holden grabbed one of the complimentary water bottles off the dresser and handed it to me.

I leaned against the wall, taking a long hard look at my travel companion as I cracked the lid and drank down half. The trip had been really eye opening. Holden was so different from the boy I taunted in high school. He was now the nicest guy I knew, and as promised, a friend to boot. My troubled past didn't seem to bother him, or at least he made me feel like it wasn't a problem. How amazing was this guy?

"Thanks again for picking up the cost." There he went, being all naturally sweet. Damn.

"Well, thank *you* for the car rental and doing all the driving." Although I would've driven over the speed limit and we would've arrived earlier, Holden was a safer driver by far. My road skills weren't at his level.

Neither of us moved, and the air crackled with an awkward pause as we gazed around the suite, as if we were unsure what to do next - although an idea or two sprung to mind.

I swallowed down a gulp of water and stretched my neck from side to side, trying to loosen the tension. "Do you mind if I take a shower?"

"Of course not. Take your time." He quickly turned away and grabbed the one suitcase he brought to the room. What was that look in his eyes? A flash of desire? Was he feeling what I was feeling? Or was I flat out exhausted, and reading too much into something that wasn't there?

Regardless, my heart twittered in anticipation as I propped my own suitcase onto the luggage holder and rifled through until I found a pair of pajamas and my toiletries. A long shower was just what I needed. Maybe even a cold one.

As I locked the bathroom door, my clothes fell to the floor in a heap. The hot water poured over my hair and body, and once I allowed the free, fragrant shampoo to wash over me and invade my senses, my thoughts wandered over to Holden.

How the frail and meekness had faded away, to be

replaced by a buff bod and handsome features I never would've guessed he'd grown into. But it was more than surface looks. It was the way his dark green eyes held my stare when I talked, like he was genuinely interested in everything I said. How he didn't run when seeing my arms, and in fact, shared space with me without judgement. Holden had become the whole package, and I was a better person for having been witness to his transformation.

I rinsed the shampoo and applied a conditioner ripe with the scent of fresh apples, breathing in the calming aroma. Long gone was the sickly stench of jet fuel and day-old body odor mixed with treehouse sweat. I was finally starting to feel like a woman again, and maybe, I was looking like one too.

Shower finished, I stared at my reflection as I ran some facial crème over my skin and brushed the tangles from my hair, allowing the soft waves to bounce along my naked shoulders. I puckered in the mirror, making what I thought was a sexy face, until I softened it and tipped my head in a sweet, yet seductive pose.

Did Holden find me as attractive as I found him? Did he desire more than just a kiss or two? I didn't want to push it, and yet, there was a deep need to explore more of him.

I imagined how different things could be had I decided to not join him on the road trip, or had I not made the choice to leave Toronto behind and board the next flight leaving across the country. It was funny how that single choice had altered my thoughts and feelings. Holden, in a weird sort of way, had made an impact on my life, and a huge one at that.

"Like a crater," I said to no one and then laughed.

A knock sounded, and I quickly grabbed a luxuriously thick towel to cover myself. "Yes?"

"Sorry to bother you, but I'm wondering if you're almost done. I really need to use the bathroom." He sounded like he was pressed against the door in anticipation.

"Oh, yes, sorry." I put my spaghetti strap pajama top on and jumped into the mismatched shorts. Gathering my things, I opened the door and allowed the remaining steam to escape.

Holden's mouth dropped.

"What?" I asked, concern on the tip of my tongue.

Yes, my scars were visible, but I thought we were past that. Mostly.

"Nothing. You just … You…" He stopped and took a quick breath. "You look different than before."

There was a charm in his words to play off. "Oh? Different better?"

"You're gorgeous," he whispered as a maroon flush deepened over his cheeks. In a rush, he stepped by me to go into the bathroom.

A grin stretched across my cheeks as deep as the burn, and I turned my head to hide what was so brazenly displayed across my face.

I'd just put my dirty things away and set out fresh

clothes for the morning when he emerged with an expression of relief.

A devilish gaze roamed the length of my body and settled back to lock eye contact. "Think I'll take a shower too."

"For sure. I'm going to head out onto the balcony and take in the view."

I pulled back the patio door and stepped outside. There was a slight breeze, but sadly not as fresh and salty as I had hoped, being so close to the ocean. The view was a little disappointing as well, with nothing interesting to settle my gaze on – no twinkling city lights and no visible stars to check out either. Guess I hadn't scored as great a deal as I'd thought; there may be no view however, at least the room was top notch. Or so it seemed.

After several minutes of nighttime skyline gazing hoping to see something remarkable, Holden emerged onto the patio in low slung pajama pants and a t-shirt. Looking effortlessly sexy. And smelling like fresh heaven.

"You're staring," he whispered into the breeze.

Immediately, I turned away, unaware of my actions. My cheeks flamed once again, and a faint rush of heat bloomed across my chest.

"I'm not upset. In fact, it's a little flattering. I never get noticed." He stood beside me, leaning against the metal railing.

"I highly doubt that." The words were out before I could stop them. "You're cute and sweet and smart. I'm sure all the girls at the university will be wild over you."

He lightly snorted. "I'd like to believe that, but I'm no fool. Girls only want the bad boys. I can't offer them an ounce of that."

Sure, it was true what they said about the appeal of a bad boy, covered in tats, shirking responsibilities, breaking the law just a little, or maybe a lot. It was a huge turn on. All my life, I'd been drawn to those types of guys, and yet, there was something refreshing about Holden. A family guy, super smart, and just a genuinely nice person through and through.

"Maybe for some girls, but not all." I found myself reaching for his hand. "There's nothing wrong with being nice."

"Nice guys finish last." His gaze danced between my eyes as the distance between us narrowed. "What about you?"

"What about me?" I swallowed and held my breath.

"You must have guys falling at your feet?"

I glanced down to my naked toes. "Not anymore."

"That's not true." He tipped my chin and stared into my soul.

Suddenly I felt naked, raw, and exposed. Like Holden, except he couldn't hide his feelings.

His Adam's apple bobbed and beneath his fingertips there was a slight tremor. If I didn't know better, he was nervous, and it was best to take the lead on the direction this suddenly felt like it was heading to.

I pushed my chest against him and looped my arms around his neck, threading my fingers through his silky, damp hair as I pulled him in close, tipping my head. Did I dare?

Lips parted, my breath catching in my throat, I stared into the depths of his dark green eyes before I tenderly brushed my lips over his.

He pulled back ever so, and his gaze searched out mine. "I really shouldn't."

"It's okay." My hands moved down his back, over the tight muscles rippling beneath the shirt. I nodded, just enough to signal I was okay.

Responding, his lips claimed mine, and he pushed against me until my shoulders connected against the cool of the patio door. Without a word, I stepped to the side, putting my feet on the warm carpet of the hotel room. Resuming his tantalizing kisses, he guided me backwards until the cotton material of the bed brushed against my calves and slowly, he lowered me onto the cloud-like comforter and stepped back, pulling his t-shirt free of his perfect, muscular body.

For a moment, he just stood there, in a worried hesitation, taking me all in.

Thinking of how inexperienced his first kisses felt, I couldn't help the thought that popped into my head, and I wasn't sure how to react if he was. "Is this your first time?"

"Hell, no." He ran a hand through his hair, a fire burning in his soulful look. "I just can't get over how beautiful you are. You really are magnificent, Iris."

I tipped my head down. No man had made me feel this way before. And it wasn't just lip service before Holden got some action like others had, there was truth ribboned through his words.

"You're the—"

Holden truly was the whole package. Smarts, personality, and one hell of a hot body.

He leaned down to kiss me, but the kiss had morphed from sweet and innocent-like, to a man in charge and full of passion. The tide had changed, and the shift was palpable.

I was in big, BIG trouble. And so was my heart.

Chapter Twelve

Our kisses deepened, and I sunk into the softness of the bed as Holden pushed himself between my legs, only two thin pieces of cloth separating an intimate and personal connection.

His hands threaded through the tangles of my damp hair as he pressed his tongue into my waiting mouth, dancing and teasing.

I wanted things to go further, and feeling this hot and bothered, I needed the relief I knew he'd bring. "Holden?"

He dragged tiny kisses along my collarbone. "Mmhmm."

"Do you have a condom?"

"No." He stopped his movements, and pulled back a bit to look into my eyes, as shock and disappointment settled in. "Do you?"

I shook my head. This wasn't planned out. Not at all.

Otherwise, I would've grabbed a box at our last stop. Or at the gift shop.

Holden lifted himself off me and flopped onto the vacant part of the bed beside me.

"Do you want this to continue?" I asked, searching his face. It didn't have to end. There were other ways, we could be creative. Oh, so creative.

Without hesitation, he nodded. "But it's a sign that I shouldn't."

"Nonsense. We're both consenting adults. I can check the gift shop. I'm sure they must sell some." I shrugged and took a deep breath.

"Then you wait right here, and I'll go check." Before I could stop him, he'd grabbed his wallet, his t-shirt off the other bed, and dashed out the door.

Taking a moment to collect my wits and to calm the erratic beat of my heart, I switched on the bathroom light, and left the door open a crack, while turning off the other lights in the room. The soft light was borderline romantic, as much as we could get in a fancy hotel room. Leaving the patio door open for a fresh breeze, I did, however, close the gauzy curtains. Not that anyone could see, but still, I wasn't about to be on full display. It was enough to let Holden in, and for him to see me with all my scars visible. In preparation, I also removed most of the pillows and rolled down the comforter, making sure the bed was as ready as I was.

Did I make it easy for him, and remove my pajama bottoms, or should I allow him to take them off in a slow seductive way? Or could I recharge the mood by playfully doing a little strip tease? I wasn't sure what he'd prefer, or which was the right way to go. I didn't want to be too eager, but he had just run for condoms. Chances were, this was going to be fast. For us both.

A knock sounded on the door, and I whipped my head around.

Holden's voice came from the other side. "I forgot the key."

"Coming," I sang as I skipped over and opened the door.

He didn't stand there long and pushed into the room. "That's something I've never done before."

I locked the door and slid the chain into place. "Really? Thought you said you've done this."

"Yeah, but she already had the protection. I've never had to buy any." He set the box down on the dresser, and fumbled it open, dumping them out. "They only had a three pack."

I almost laughed at the hopefulness in his voice. Almost. Since we were parting ways tomorrow, three would likely be enough.

He threw the box in the garbage, covered it with a few tissues and tossed his hands out to the side when he connected with my stare.

"I don't need the housekeeping staff to know."

I stepped closer, desperately needing him to stop talking. "It's no biggie. I'm sure they see it all the time." I caressed his cheek, still soft and barely a hint of stubble, and planted a teasing kiss upon his trembling lips. "Now where were we?"

"You were there, on the bed, and I was, umm, kind of…" His Adam's apple bobbed and a faint blush coloured his cheeks.

"Like this?" I sat on the bed and scooted back, putting a little space between my knees.

The wanton desire flicked back to his face after he focused on my throbbing center and pressed out against his pajama bottoms. "Yeah, umm, like that."

"And where were you?" I purred and made a come here motion with my finger.

"I, uh."

I pressed my lips to him, to silence him, but mostly to kill the lingering awkwardness. All I needed was a half-minute, and we'd be back on track. Opening up, Holden slipped between my legs and balanced himself on one arm as his left hand grazed my cheek and trailed down my neck to settle on my boob. Through the fabric, he held me and gently squeezed, and the speed of his tongue told me how excited he was, but it was the occasional twitch that spoke louder. He may have done this before, but it was maybe once. Or twice. I was going to have to guide him. However, I was ready to be his instructor.

I rolled myself into a sitting position, and expertly pulled my top off, my perky nipples on full display. He pushed me back onto the bed and moved his finger all around the swell of my breast, circling closer and closer to the nipple, but never actually touching it. He did the same with the other one, albeit a little slower, more seductively, and way more tantalizing.

I let him explore, and his hand moved further south, but his mouth zeroed in on my breast, and the heat from it nearly pushed me over. His tongue flicked against my nipple, and I dug my hands into the bedding in sweet ecstasy.

Not wanting to be the only one driven crazy, I moved my hand down over his chest – that I needed to come back and exam in more detail – and settled over the visibly excited part of him. Through his bottoms, I rubbed and wrapped my hand around him.

"Oh, sweet Jesus." His breath was hot against my breasts. "One thing at a time." His fingers teased along the edge of my waistband, and I lifted my hips. Palm side down, he inched under the elastic, and smoothly over my stomach on a direct path to…

Oh my god.

He cupped my mound, pushing a finger between my lips, and dove right in. One finger. Then another. His palm rubbed against me, until he slowly pulled his damp fingers higher, finding my sweet spot and circling all around it.

"Holden." My breath caught in my throat.

"That feel good?" His gaze locked on mine.

"So good." I could barely breathe. Instead, I gripped him a little tighter, and allowed my thumb to mimic his actions. Slowly, I caressed his tip and listened as he gasped and groaned in a deep, sexy growl. "Two can play this game."

He rolled between my legs and as he slithered down, planting hot, wet kisses on my rib cage, my naval, and back up quickly to each breast while his hands gripped the edge of my bottoms, and slipped them down to my knees. "So gorgeous."

He held the shorts as I slowly pulled out a leg, leaving one bare and as exposed as my core. His focus moved to take in the scene as I slowly moved my hand over myself.

"You like it there?"

I danced my fingers overtop, while my other hand settled over a nipple and rubbed it. I knew what I liked, and I was going to show Holden the way to make me fall apart.

Kneeling between my legs, he tenderly ran his hands up the inside of my thighs, stopping short of my pleasure zone. His hands moved over my hip bones, leaving his thumbs to find my sweet spot and rub it in circular motions, intensifying the pressure on each deliberate pass. Slowly, he planted kisses along my inner thigh, inching closer and closer until his tongue replaced the deft work of his thumbs. Hot and velvety, he flicked and rubbed and wiggled, until I couldn't hold back any longer, and like a rocket lifting off the launch pad, I was a goner, and my emotional state wasn't far behind.

I pulled his shirt free of his body, desperate to get the man inside me, and with my toes, I looped them into the waistband of his pajamas and pushed them down.

"Impressive," he said, reaching for a foil packet we'd tossed onto the bed.

"I haven't even begun yet." I cocked an eyebrow and took the condom from his hand, tearing the packet with my teeth. "Please, allow me."

He swallowed, and for a heartbeat of a moment, I worried I was coming on too strong, but when I looked up into his dark green eyes, the worry faded just as fast – there was a tantalizing grin stretched from one side to the other. He stepped closer, and while I slowly rolled the condom over his impressive length, I kept my gaze locked on his long lashes and the heated expression dancing in the depths of his soul.

I slowly lowered myself back against the softness of the cloud.

Holden climbed onto the bed and resumed kissing up my naval, over the fast pace of my heart, and settled into the crook of my neck. He lowered himself between my legs, fumbling as he found the sweet spot and pushed himself inside. Pulling back, he gazed into my eyes and was about to speak, but I drew him close and sealed his lips with mine as we joined into one unit. Together, we moved in a perfect rhythm, our tongues dancing in the sweet taste of sex as our bodies bashed together in a frenzied motion. In and out. Pumping and grinding. Breathing and gasping. I wrapped my legs around his waist, locking together at the ankles, and gripped him tighter with each thrust, pulling my ass higher.

"Oh, Jesus." He grunted and groaned, and with a fast rush to the finish, he let out a deep guttural growl. "Oh, good Lord."

I took his full weight for a breath until he collected himself, and rolled beside me, kissing my shoulder.

"That was…" His breath was furious, and there was a change in the lightness of his eyes. However, it was the tenderness in his voice that wrapped around my soul and gave it a gentle squeeze. "Thank you."

"Thank *you*." I pressed my back against his hard chest.

Holden wrapped his arm around me, putting more kisses onto my shoulder and the side of my neck. "That was amazing. You are amazing."

"Told you." I giggled a little.

I loved having his arms wrapped around me, that feeling of having been totally exposed and vulnerable, and yet, somehow protected, needed, and the best part – wanted. Tomorrow was going to hurt a whole lot.

* * *

To use one of Holden's big words, there was something ethereal about waking up in his embrace. Although sleep had claimed me for less time than he had, I'd never felt more rested. After another shower, we left the hotel room hand in hand before nine and headed to the ferry terminal.

Holden drove our rental into the long lineup awaiting boarding. "Ever been on a ferry before?"

"Pretty much every single thing I've done on this trip has been a first."

From a last-minute plane trip, to making a new friend, the road trip, the treehouse, the hotel, and to giving him a piece of my heart with my secrets I'd never given another soul – they were all firsts.

"It's awesome – a unique way to see Vancouver. You'll love it."

A dull headache formed as a sinking feeling gurgled in my stomach. Holden had missed the meaning of my statement. Did he really feel the same as I did? Or was last night just a way for his itch to be scratched? Maybe he wasn't as wholesome as I'd thought.

Turning away, I counted the cars ahead of us, sitting in a silence I wasn't sure how to address. Holden was head bopping to a song only he could hear, while his hands tapped against the steering wheel. Birds circled high above in the clear blue skies, and vehicle by vehicle, it was our turn to drive onto the darkened cave of the giant boat. It was like staring at a cruise ship, huge and magnificent.

"You're awfully quiet."

"Just trying to memorize it all." But it was a lie, and I swallowed down a lump in the back of my throat; the kind that grows just before a heartbreaking cry.

In less than two hours, we'd be parting ways, and I wasn't sure how to prepare for it.

He smiled, but it lacked the zest and calmness it usually sported. "We'll be able to walk around. Truly check it out, although it's not that exciting. We'll have roughly ninety minutes to explore, or just sit, veg, and enjoy our time together."

Ninety final minutes. One hundred and twenty until we separated at the airport, so he could go home to his grandparents and Amber's friend would fly me away to Cheshire Bay.

My heart plummeted and a numbness that was hard to ignore washed over me and threatened to pull me under.

He drove the car onto the boat, and once the vehicle was in position, we were free to roam, along with the other passengers who were flooding the holding deck.

Following the crowd, we quietly ascended a set of metal stairs and strolled the outer deck, heading toward the bow of the ship.

Despite the sudden melancholy in my soul, my jaw dropped at the incredible view and it coloured my greying mood. "Wow."

Pale blue-grey ocean with flecks of white diamonds glittered out as far as the eye could see, and puffy, snow-white clouds dotted the horizon. The morning sun was magnificently bright, so I shielded my eyes as we wandered the deck.

Unsure if I should hold his hand and prolong the incoming hurt, or if I should just start wrapping my heart in bandages, I twisted away, pulling deep into my jacket as I zipped it close. My hair blew across my eyes from the crisp, salty air as I tried to avoid the man eclipsing the sunshine.

"It's really gorgeous. Breathtaking really."

"I agree." But he wasn't looking at the ocean, or the flock of circling birds, or the lush green islands, he was staring straight at me. Tenderly, he brushed a tendril of wavy hair off my face. Under his breath, he whispered, barely loud enough for me to hear. "You're the one I should be with."

"Stop, please. You'll just make things worse." My voice lowered as the heat singed, and I was thankful for the cool breeze to help tame it as I turned away to stop him from seeing the sadness creeping into my everything. "You and I know both know what happens when we get across this stretch of water."

He nuzzled into my back, and his words were as far off as if he'd yelled them from the other side of the ship. "There's so much I want to tell you, and there's so much I can't. This is killing me."

I inhaled a lungful of the ocean air, desperately tried to keep my unstable emotions in check, but the start of a crack surfaced in my words. "Me too."

There was no comforting embrace or friendly expression. No words of encouragement. Our time was ticking down, and maybe like me, he didn't know how to move forward from that.

With each painful step towards the bow, I deepened the crevasse growing between us. I approached a railing and leaned away, staring blindly into the depths of the blue-grey waters lapping against the hull.

Voices milled all around, a mixture of excitement and incoming boredom, but most jockeyed for a position to watch the ship leave the dock. It was getting crowded, and a suffocating claustrophobia started to hover.

A loud air horn sounded, and I nearly jumped the railing to the car deck below, but Holden had the foresight to grab hold of me a second before.

"Should've warned you. Sorry."

My knuckles turned white from the death grip I gave the ice-cold railing.

"Here we go." He boxed me in and kissed my shoulder when the boat shuddered and rocked as it cast off from the terminal.

"What about your grandparents?" Suddenly chilled to the bones from the breeze, I huddled deeper into my jacket and pulled my hands into the sleeves.

"Right." He pulled out his phone and made a quick call.

The conversation went by again without a mention of me, or of him having travelled with anyone, but rather than start a fight and end on a low note, I let it slide. Instead, I texted Amber and waited for her response.

Holden ended the call with a whisp of excitement. "Less than two hours, and I'll be home. Finally. Made it in the nick of time. Tonight, I'll be out observing, and tomorrow—"

"You'll be able to start your new career." My voice collapsed under the weight of the future.

It was hard to believe how much had happened over the course of a couple of days, even less than that, really. The past thirty-three hours had felt like a week or more.

"Yeah," his voice solemn and weak. "My new life awaits me. It's everything I've ever wanted, right?"

It was a rhetorical question, as his gaze flew off me and went as far away as possible. The light was gone in his eyes, and his shoulders rolled forward from an imaginary weight bringing him down. I was sure by this point, he'd be thrilled about the new beginnings. He'd worked so hard to achieve all his goals, they were within his grasp. Why the sudden change of heart?

He cleared his throat, and quickly turned to me. "What

about you? What are you going to do when you get to your cousin's home?"

I shrugged, my gaze focusing on anything but the sadness in his dull green eyes; the sparkle diminished with each passing minute. "All I'd thought about was getting away from Toronto. I'd never really pictured what I'd be doing if I finally succeeded."

Thirty-six hours ago, *that* had been my only goal. To escape all the hurt, pain, and loneliness I'd shouldered and endured. For a few hours, I'd been free of it all. Never figured being this far away from it, it would somehow find me again.

"You're across the country, so I'd say you succeeded." There was a hint of pride in his voice, but it was the distanced look in his eyes haunting me more, and I tore myself away.

There was a gentle swaying motion to the boat, and over the speakers, music played.

Holden reached for my hand, and I placed it in his. He wrapped his hand around my waist and pulled me closer, moving in time to the beat.

"Here?" I asked. We weren't really going to dance here, in front of people. This wasn't a bar.

"Why not?"

"Because it's not, I don't know, proper?"

"So what? Let's live for this moment. Let me memorize everything about you. Like you are doing."

Which was true. I was trying to take as many mental

pictures as possible. I huddled against him, pulling his hand in close to my chest as he held me tight. We swayed and shuffled our feet, and I inhaled ever moment. The firm way his arm wrapped around me, and the gentle position of his hand on my lower back. The softness of the sweater my cheek was leaning on, thick enough to absorb the tears I couldn't hold back. The way his jaw pressed against my forehead, like we'd been a couple forever, and not just a few hours.

It killed part of my soul to realize how happy I'd been with Holden, and how perfectly at peace I'd been. I had been who I was, and not what someone needed me to be, and he'd been completely accepting of that.

In less than two hours, we'd be going our separate ways. Despite being relatively close distance wise, an island still stretched between us; me on the west side, him on the east. A five-hour drive at least. Hardly easy for a weekend hookup, especially with his work hours at the observatory.

"We skipped breakfast, and I'm getting hungry. Do you want anything to eat or drink?"

My appetite had long since disappeared into a mass of knots, so I shook my head.

"Okay, no problem. Can I hold you?"

The ribbon of pain in his request hurt to hear, and in not wanting the fantasy to end, I allowed him to wrap his arms around me and I breathed him in.

It was comforting to be held, even as heartache

threatened to crack me in half, and try as I may, my intense feelings for Holden were not disappearing. My work was going to be cut out for me when the time came. I'd been foolish in letting the barriers around my heart take a couple of solid hits.

The mainland coastline became more distant as we crossed the strait, and the numerous islands we were going to skirt around dotted the horizon ahead of us. We walked to a vacant seat at the front of the ship and cozied together, one last time. The crisp air cooled the space around us, but maybe it was because I was putting on the chill.

His brows furrowed, and he stared without expression.

Was he thinking about what would happen when we'd arrive on the island? Was his heart constricting, and trying to hold itself together like mine was?

Travelling to Cheshire Bay was supposed to be a trip, not an expedition, and yet, here I was having reconnected with a classmate and finding feelings developing that had no right to blossom. I wasn't fit to be with anyone, at least not long term. Mentally and emotionally, I was a wreck and a disaster of epic proportions. How could I foolishly believe the spark igniting between us was something special, and not just a product of being forced together on this journey?

And yet...

Holden had given me something I didn't know I'd needed – true friendship. He saw me for more than who I had been, and despite my intellectual inferiority, he saw me as an equal. I had more fun with him over the past two days than I'd had in a long time and had found a deeper connection with him than any of my past relationships. He had the uncanny ability to ease my pain and forget my troubles. He saw the scars, but it only bothered him in an emotional sense, not of the physical scarring, but of the mental hurt.

Knowing that caused the pain in the depths of my heart to blister.

My left palm was tender with crescent moons from my clenched fists. At least it was pain I had control over. There was no control over the ache building in my chest as we inched toward the end.

Our final stop came into view, and I swallowed down the solid lump growing firmer and larger in the back of my throat. The finish line was near. Too near. I fought to hold back the forthcoming tears.

I recrossed my legs and leaned my back against his chest. "How far from the ferry to your grandparents?"

"If I didn't drive you to the airport?"

I nodded, confused by his question.

"Two minutes?" He pointed to the right of the terminal as we coasted along. "My grandparent's house is on the edge there. Grandma's probably on the deck watching right now."

I scanned the houses wondering what she looked like, and if she was indeed watching. "Can you see her?"

"Nah, but she'll be able to see the ship. It's hard to ignore."

"She'll be expecting you within minutes as soon as you dock?" Little flickers of envy flared in my gut. He was almost home.

"Grandpa's picking me up from the airport, as I still need to drop off the rental. Did Amber tell you what time your flight is?"

I hadn't thought to check, and quickly retrieved my phone. In my messages was the ticket I needed to get through security and out onto the tarmac.

"In about an hour. There was a vacant seat."

"We'll make it just in time." He may have smiled, but it wasn't the kind that pushed his cheeks high against his eyes. It was trimmed in pain, and hard to look at.

Like the coward I suddenly felt I'd become, I stared at the ferry dock which we were rapidly gaining ground upon. "We should get into the car, so we're ready to clear out."

He reached out his hand, but I pocketed it instead. "You okay?"

"Just trying to make this easier." I started to walk away, pushing past a couple and then a young family.

"Make what easier?" He pulled me to a standstill.

"Us separating. Saying goodbye."

The breeze rippled his hair after he ran his hand through it, but his lips stayed firmly shut.

"We need to go. Your grandparents are waiting, and I have a flight to catch."

Remembering the way back to the holding deck, I dragged myself down to the end-to-end line of vehicles on the deck below, and maneuvering between the cars, stood in front of ours.

A signal from the remote unlocked the doors, and I slid into the warmth of the interior. No breeze in here. No crisp ocean air either. Rather, it hinted of the apple-scented conditioner I'd used this morning, after my shower, after using the third and final condom.

Silently, Holden slipped behind the wheel and started the car just enough to put the radio on.

Some form of a cosmic joke was upon us, as once again the Goo Goo Dolls song *Iris* came on. Immediately, I pounded the off button and fought the incoming wave of tears.

The gentle swaying of the boat came to a stop as we docked at the northern tip of Victoria. It was time to deboard the ferry and head to my next destination - the airport leading me to my new home and away from Holden deLauer.

One by one, the vehicles drove off the boat and onto the ramp, until we joined them and headed away from what had been the most incredible journey I'd ever been on.

Barely on the island, it was easy to remark on the physical differences between the mainland and here. The landscape was filled with towering trees and serenity instead of high-rises and a bustling metropolis feel. Holden had warned me how different the island was, and he was right. My own personal feelings were also as different.

We passed a marina – a tiny town named Sidney – and before I had any time to truly prepare for the separation, we'd quickly turned off the main road on approach to the airport. Just like that, my time with Holden was done.

It hurt to breathe.

Splinters formed across my heart.

My vision blurred as he drove over to the loading zone in front of the building and shut the engine down.

Silent as he'd been since the ferry, he hopped out at the same time as I did and met me at the trunk.

First my suitcase, then my backpack, he set them on the ground and kicked at the pebbles scattered around.

Unsure of how to end things, I inhaled slowly, taking a long lingering look at my travel companion. Rather than embrace him in a hug of a lifetime, like every fiber of my being suggested, I thrust out my hand to shake his.

Holden stared wide-eyed. "Seriously?"

I nodded while making a tight fist with my left hand, and again, deeply dug my nails into my palms. Feeling the sharp, stinging pain was preferable to the unrelenting aches stabbing me in the chest. "It's better this way."

"You're actually serious?" He didn't even blink.

I shrugged and took a backwards step. If I didn't act fast,

the dam was going to burst all down my face and turn me into a blubbering mess, and I couldn't leave us looking so wrecked. "You and I both know this was all because of the situation. Imagine if we hadn't encountered the smoke – we both know we wouldn't be standing here."

"That's the beauty of this thing we call life. Sometimes it throws a huge kink into your plans. Especially the ones you can do nothing to change." He sent a pebble flying across the parking lot.

I grabbed my backpack and flung it over my shoulder where it smacked me in the back. "What can't you change? Why do you keep saying shit like that?"

His body went ramrod straight, and he avoided looking at me. Even his voice and tone changed to something cold and heartless. "You're right, okay. We happened as a product of our circumstances. It would've never happened otherwise. A girl like you, a guy like me, in the real world–" He waved a hurtful finger between us. "This doesn't happen."

"But…" I swallowed as the single word dangled in the air.

This wasn't happening, it couldn't be.

Crevasses replaced the cracks, and the bigger the split, the more the pain rippled through.

I inhaled sharply and tried my damnedest to make my words light and cheerful, even if feeling them was the furthest thing from the truth. "Maybe, one day, you'll be able to look back on this time with a smile, and not such a detached obligation, like I'm suddenly getting from you. You'll be able to tell your grandkids all about your weekend travel escapades to this amazing new job you'd waited your whole life for, and all the big dreams you'd planned, and maybe you'll sit in your rocker on your front porch in a glossed over glaze wondering *whatever happened to that girl*? In a few months, weeks, or even days, you'll forget all about me, and you'll forget my name. I'll be this mere speck of time in your life."

He took a step back and swayed slightly while rubbing his forehead and shaking his head.

"And that's okay. I'll be okay with that." I nodded, as if I needed to do so to honestly believe it myself. "It's all I am, just a faded memory to most people. A chapter of a book they'd rather never read again."

His voice broke, and he reached for me. "That's not true at all. You're a book I want to know more about. I'd still be in Calgary if you hadn't suggested the car."

"You're smart, you would've figured it out."

He shrugged. "Perhaps. But dang it. You and I, we're a great team. This isn't fair. None of this is fair, god damn it."

A sad chagrin nestled onto my lips. Tears built fast as my heart fractured. A million ideas ran through my head, most were nonsensical, but a couple could work. For luck, I threw them out into the world. "Maybe in a few months, once I'm on my feet, I can visit, and we can hang out? Or was that friends thing all a lie?"

As Holden's face morphed into confusion, then reluctance, and I regretted saying anything. I should've kept my foolish lips sealed. It would've hurt less.

"God, I want this so bad. I want *you* so bad." His Adam's apple bobbed with his audible swallow. "But a few months from now will be too late."

Then, like a two by foot to the head, it blindsided me, and I kicked myself for having been so stupid. The air crackled until I punctured it with my high-pitched laugh; one of those uncomfortable, heart-breaking sounds. It all made sense.

"Oh. My. God. You have a girlfriend, right? I should've known. That's why you couldn't tell your grandparents you were travelling with anyone."

Chapter Thirteen

My eyes widened, and I smacked his shoulder with my raw and scratched up palms as a deep-seated anger ignited my instarage. "Jesus fucking Christ." My voice rose an octave. "I'm the other woman. AGAIN." I yelled as my hands flailed through the air.

A small crowd started forming as people stopped and stared.

Holden's face turned white, and his expression fell to the ground.

"You cheated on her. WITH ME. After everything I told you about what happened, you fucking used me." My blood boiled and my stomach curdled. I was going to throw up all over the parking lot.

"You don't understand."

"Fuck you." Widening the distance, I took a step back and grabbed the cracked luggage handle while hot rivers of tears flooded across my cheeks. My middle finger popped out as I spun around and stormed away.

The gathered crowd shot daggers in Holden's direction, and part of me soared as my feelings had been vindicated.

"Iris, don't leave." His voice circled around me as his own voice pitched in volume. "It's not what you think. I didn't cheat on anyone. I don't have a girlfriend. I'm not married. But, yes, I am spoken for."

I stopped at the main entrance to the airport and raised my face to the sky. "Are you fucking serious?"

Pebbles beneath Holden's feet scratched on the concrete as he approached, murmurs rippled through the crowd.

His voice lowered. "Before you walk out of my life, you need to hear the truth. My grandparents are seriously old-fashioned. Like from the turn of the century old-fashioned. They were an arranged marriage, and Grandma only met Grandpa a few weeks before their wedding day."

I swiped my sleeve under my eyes. I wanted to move on. I wanted to refuse to hear him out, but my feet were suddenly frozen to the ground, and I hated myself – that I didn't have the strength to leave him behind. I hated how his lowered voice had a power over me I didn't understand.

He got closer but dismissed the crowd with a wave. "My mother was the only child of that arrangement. Romance and courting were completely absent. Of my parents four or five get-to-know-you dates, they were pre-approved by Grandpa, who was also in attendance, and their marriage was practically an arranged marriage in and of itself, even though it worked out in the end."

With his lowered voice, and the heat of the moment tampered, the small crowd broke up.

I sighed with a morsel of relief. I wasn't an attraction, and I hated being the center of attention. As the air cooled further, I dug my nails into my sore palms and closed my eyes.

He had stepped close enough I heard his laboured breathing. "In an attempt to break the cycle, my parents moved out east, to get out from under the pressure, as my grandparents controlled everything. It failed. They failed. Miserably. When I was young, my parents enlisted in my grandparents help for our education and upbringing, under certain requirements. Like it or not, I must abide by their rules. All of them."

I spun back on my heels and blinked him into view, squaring my shoulders with what little strength I had left. "What exactly are you saying? Although I think I can jump there on my own, I need to hear the truth from you."

His chin tucked in, and his focus floated somewhere over my shoulder. "I'll meet my betrothed for the first time on my twenty-third birthday. Next month."

As in an arranged marriage? His wife-to-be was already hand-picked? What in the fresh hell was that all about?

"Holy shit, Holden. This isn't the 1900s." Still stunned,

I was unable to keep my tongue in check. "You should be allowed to date *and marry* whoever you want."

"It's not that easy. You see, my sister messed everything up. When she got pregnant, she was instantly cut off. Despite her beauty and intelligence, she wasn't pure anymore, and she was worthless. The family who she was arranged to marry into dropped her. Not to be outdone, my grandparents outcasted her as well. And it wasn't just them…" He inhaled and let out a painful breath while he shook his head. "But sadly, my parents did too. They had no choice."

"Your parents?" Talk about old-fashioned. "Everyone has a choice."

He shrugged, but it wasn't as robust as before – it was like he was shouldering the weight of the world. "Now I'm the prize, so to speak. I have the chance to right all the wrongs. Although I've yet to meet her, I'm told Dahlia is a perfect match and will strengthen our family line. She comes from an extensive heritage of opulence and grace, and her family is willing to overlook the blackmark within my own. Our future is all planned out." There was no enthusiasm in his voice, not even a hint. He got more excited about a rock on the ground than he did over his future bride. "With this requirement, my grandparents have provided me a healthy living allowance, and I transfer a portion of it to my sister." He paused and his gaze searched my face. "No one, aside from you, has ever known that."

What a life, and what a guy. He was sacrificing his own wants and needs for his sister.

"As long as I follow the rules, which includes marrying my betrothed, that money will keep coming, and I can make sure Myriam is taken care of for as long as possible."

I nodded, trying to absorb all that he was saying. "It sounds so unbelievable. I don't know what to make of it all."

My anger had long sailed away with his confession, replaced with sadness and pain and utter hopelessness. No matter what we wanted, what I wanted, it would never happen. We'd been doomed from the beginning.

"I know it sounds crazy, but I didn't tell you because at first, it was pointless. We were just sitting side by side on what should've been a standard flight. Once we landed in Calgary, things changed. I wanted to say something, but I didn't know how. It's not something that comes up in conversation."

Somewhere behind me, a jet roared to life.

I stomped my foot. "It should've. At least before you jumped into the sack with me."

"I wanted to, believe me, but I got swept away in the moment."

"Whatever." I rolled my eyes.

"You're not so perfect either."

"At least I know I have faults." I pulled up my sleeves and flashed my arms. "Believe me, I know all about them. But here's the difference between you and me – I never hid them.

When you asked, I was upfront and didn't try to hide anything. It wasn't pleasant, but at least I said something. And I'm trying to be better and I'm trying to do better. I'm trying to not repeat the same mistakes, and it's so hard. It's a daily battle between my mind and my heart." I pointed to my head and then to my chest, hoping to nail it home. "I'm learning what's important, what's valuable, what's worth fighting for. And you? Have you ever decided to stand up to your family's archaic rules? All your life you've been pushed around and bullied, and here you are still being told what to do. They're holding their power and wealth over you, and you cower to their form of bullying. In all these years, you haven't learned a god-damn thing, have you?"

"It's not like that at all, and I wish you understood. I wish I had more time to truly explain the whole thing, but I don't. You just don't understand how families work." He huffed and puffed out his chest.

"Ouch. Thanks a lot."

"Jesus, that came out wrong." He gripped his hand around my wrist, sympathy rolling off him in waves. "I wish I was as vocal as you, and I wish it wouldn't destroy my family to tell them all about our weekend together. These past two days have been the best of my life, and I'm in shock how somehow, over the past thirty-sixish hours, I've fallen for you."

The knife in my heart twisted to the left. It didn't matter

what it meant; it was how it was said that hurt. "Thanks for including the word *somehow* in your little declaration as if it's a miracle how a guy like you and a girl like me could ever happen."

He threw his hands out to the side of his body. "Jesus, you said it yourself. We're two different people."

I wrapped my hands tightly around my achy chest. "Because I'm trying to protect what's left of my fucking heart, Holden. It doesn't matter what I felt, or what you *somehow* managed to feel. It can never happen; you're betrothed to another." Hot tears streamed down over my cheeks, but this time, I didn't care if he saw them.

"Iris." His voice a mere whisper in the wind as his face fell along with his tone.

I smeared the tears and blinked away the blurry view. "Just once, I'd like for things to be easy, to not have everything be such a continuous and arduous battle, and I can't fight for something I'll never get. You may be so God-damned book smart you leapt ahead of your peers in education, but you lack street smarts and common sense. At least I know when I've lost. You just keep adding salt to the wound."

"But..."

"As much as I..." The words balled up in a lump, lodged into my throat. "I need to go. Goodbye, Holden. Enjoy your perfect life."

Chapter Fourteen

Deflated and heartbroken beyond anything I'd ever felt before, I stepped off the plane in Cheshire Bay. A whiff of salty air mixed with jet fuel swirled about, making me more nauseated than I wanted to be, perhaps it was from all the crying I'd done as we flew across the island.

Amber raced over when both my feet touched the asphalt of the tarmac.

"You're here." She wrapped her arms around me, and I melted into the embrace.

My strength threatened to puddle the longer she held me.

"Thank you, Eric." She spoke over my shoulder to the pilot and then turned her focus back to me. "What's wrong? Was it a rough flight?"

The pilot spoke from behind us and softly put his hand on my shoulder, patting gently. "Smooth flight. I think it's the exhaustion of her turbulent weekend travels."

What? He knows? Shit.

"Sorry, I'm not used to air travel." It was the only excuse I was going to allow to leak out. No one, except maybe Amber eventually, needed to know my heart was broken. "Thanks for sending your friend to come and pick me up. Sorry it was such a delay."

"Eric was more than happy to help. I'm just glad you're safe, and you're home."

I'm home?

Like a big sister, or with a motherly kind of affection, she wiped away my tears and looked over my shoulder. "Your bags are just coming off the plane. Let's grab them and get you unpacked."

I followed Amber as she walked over to the luggage being loaded onto a flat deck dolly.

"Which are yours?"

There were only five bags being unloaded. My two, and one each for the other three passengers who flew with us.

"The pink one and the back pack."

The baggage handler laughed. "Ah, the one that feels like it's loaded with rocks."

"Mitch, be nice." Amber stopped and introduced us. "This is my dear friend, Iris Charbonneau, a new transplant from Ontario. Iris, this is my best friend's husband, Mitch. You'll meet Cedar inside."

"Welcome to Cheshire Bay." Mitch extended his hand, which I reciprocated.

The pilot walked over and joined us, leading me to believe I was surrounded by a connected group of besties.

I reached for my luggage after exchanging pleasantries.

"No, please. Let me take them." Mitch grabbed the cart. "I'll meet you out front, after I take these to their rightful owners. Go say hi to Cedar before she has a heart attack."

We turned, and there in the bank of windows was a beautiful blonde, who dashed through the door and sprang over to us. "Oh my god, you must be Iris."

Before I had a chance to put some distance between us, she embraced me in a deep hug.

"I'm so glad you're here. Amber has told us so much about you. Welcome. Welcome. Welcome. I just know you're just going to love it here." She unlatched from me and guided us to the door while spewing more highlights about Cheshire Bay than a visitor's guide.

In the span of a few minutes, I'd already been more warmly welcomed than I had my entire existence back in Toronto. Maybe there was something to this ocean air and island lifestyle.

Cedar and Eric followed us outside to the parking lot.

"Bonfire tonight." Eric stated in my direction as he loaded one of my bags into the back of Amber's jeep. "If you're feeling up to it, we'd love to have you join us."

167

I looked at Amber. Not even on the ground for twenty minutes and my social calendar already had possibilities, what was this place?

She smiled so warmly it put me at ease. "It's completely your call. We all know you've had a rough time getting here, and you want to unpack and settle in. But the company is great, the food is plentiful, and drinks are never ending."

Damn. My kryptonite. She almost had me.

"Can I think about it?" I didn't want to say no, right off the bat, especially when Amber and Eric had gone to so much trouble to get me here, but I did want a moment to catch my breath.

Eric clapped me on the shoulder. "No worries. My wife will be there, as will her sister and fiancé. Just a small intimate grouping of nine."

"Actually, it'll only be eight if she comes." Amber piped. "Antonio has been delayed. Should be here tomorrow." She raised her crossed fingers in the air. Her face lit up with her fiancé's name, and I hoped she'd share the details on how they met and all that jazz.

"It's a beautiful night." Cedar wrapped an arm around Mitch. "Hope you can come and meet the rest of the gang. They're all excited to meet you."

Stunned wouldn't even be the right word as I flipped my gaze over to Amber.

"Sorry." She shrugged with an impish grin. "I'm excited

to have you here. You sounded like you need a fresh start, and this place is perfect. Ask Lily and Mona tonight. Both were big city girls, and now, they can't imagine living anywhere else."

I stared at the four people, talking to me as if they'd know me all their lives. "Is the whole town like this?"

Amber closed the back of her jeep. "Pretty much. You'll see."

* * *

Amber poked her head into the spare room, which had now become my room. "Can I help you with anything?"

"I'm good, thanks. You've already done so much."

She walked over and sat on the queen-sized bed. "What are friends for?"

Friends. That's what Holden had said we'd always be, and he'd truly gone out of his way to prove it. Right up until the end, when he pretty much stated that's all it would *ever* be.

A familiar dull ache returned to tighten its grip around my heart.

"If you ever want to talk about what happened back home, I'm all ears. You were pretty vague, and only said you needed a fresh start."

I owed her that much after all she'd done for me.

"Well…"

Slowly, I unzipped the larger suitcase and placed a few things into the nearby dresser as I tried to find the best words to use. None came to mind. It was spill it or seal it shut.

"Brock cheated on me."

Amber's face fell and her shoulders rolled inward. "Some men aren't worth the air they breathe. They're filthy, disgusting pigs."

I snorted because it was true. Some men were.

"But that's not the worst of it. My so-called friends," and I air-quoted the word friends, "every single one of them knew what he was doing, and no one bothered to tell me. When the truth surfaced, they figured I already knew and didn't care, or they didn't know how to tell me. Some friends, right?"

I stood at the foot of my bed, holding a small stack of sweaters.

Amber rose and grabbed a few hangers, passing one to me. "Damn, that really sucks. Weren't you living with him, too?"

"I was, and then I moved back into my car. Homeless again. But it only worked for a little while until I snapped at work and lost my job." I placed a hanger through the neck of my favourite sweater. It had been a great find at the thrift store.

"Jesus. Homeless and jobless? I didn't know it was so bad. I'm so sorry."

I shrugged, the bitter memories of that week flashing

back. So raw and so new… and yet, somehow it seemed like a lifetime ago.

"Then it happened, the catalyst of life change, as the hospital psychiatrist mentioned. I downed a bottle of Fireball, drove around, and crashed my car into a tree in the ditch." I was beyond grateful to not have injured anyone else in my stupidity. "Maybe in hindsight, it was a suicide attempt, I can't recall as I really wasn't in the right state of mind. But the shattered glass on my lap helped it to become one – the easiest way to end the misery of being friendless, jobless, and homeless. I slashed my wrists real good." I pulled up the sleeve for a little show and tell. "But I passed out before I could finish the job properly."

Amber covered her mouth. "Oh, Iris."

I put another hanger through a sweater and hung it in the closet. A numbness vined its way around my heart. "I spent four days in the hospital, but it gave me time to think."

There wasn't anything else to do. I wasn't entertaining company as I had no visitors, and I was in a private room with no other roommates and a television that only picked up the free channels. Thinking was the only thing I *could* do.

"That's when you reached out to me."

One week ago.

"I took it as a sign. A chance to start fresh. Where no one knows what an utter, unlovable failure I am, until now." The numbness washed away and, in its wake, left my heart slashed wide open; I was no longer in control of my feelings. Tears burst forth, like a damn breaking. Even saying it was like a knife chopping up the remnants of my heart.

Amber tore the clothes from my hand and wrapped me in the biggest hug I've ever had. "You are not a failure, and you are loved. I love you, and trust me, I wouldn't have offered my place if I didn't. My friends, who don't even know you, love you already."

"How's that even possible?"

"Because they're the kind of people who are good right to their core, and kindness radiates out of them like sunlight through the clouds." She wiped away my tears. "Lily especially. She has a checkered past, and she came here to start fresh, much like you. She found her people here, and I trust you will too. Back in Toronto, those weren't your people, because true friends would never have treated you the way they did. Never. And Brock? I have half a mind to fly there and kick his sorry ass until he's black and blue and begging for mercy."

I laughed as the hot river of loneliness streamed down my cheeks. I couldn't imagine my tiny friend kicking Brock's ass. He was a hulking tower of a man.

"Tell me about this travel companion of yours?" She arched her brow, but not in a suspicious way. There was an element of concern in the way her expression softened and her grip around me relaxed.

However, thinking of the weekend split my heart right in half once more. "Holden was a special kind of companion."

"How so?" She motioned for me to sit on the bed as she grabbed a chair.

Without hesitation, I unloaded all the details, except the intimate ones. High school, what he'd been through, the growing attraction, and sadly, how he was predestined to another.

"It sounds like he really is a special someone." A small, pained smirk teased her lips. "I'm sorry it didn't work out."

"It was never going to happen – he's 100% unattainable. It's like someone doesn't want me to be happy." I cast my gaze to the heavens, although I didn't really believe in all that. There had been no God who saved me, or helped me, or prevented me from finding inner peace and all that mumbo-jumbo.

I ran my hand over the edge of the suitcase, peering in at the items I still had to unpack. I tipped my head to the side and stared, blinking repeatedly at the slight sparkle in the bottom of the luggage. Pushing the socks aside, I saw it – the speckled rock Holden had picked out while we were at the Enchanted Garden, where we had our first kiss.

"What's that?" Amber asked, inching her chair closer.

"Holden's rock." I sagged into the bed and gripped it in my palm, bringing it close to my chest. "He picked it out to add it to his collection. Every meaningful place he stops at, he finds a special rock or pebble, something tangible to hold onto and remember."

"Wouldn't a picture be better?"

"We have those too." But I wondered if he didn't delete his, erasing the trip, and therefore me, from his existence.

"Wonder why he gave you the rock?"

I shook my head, not knowing the answer myself. Perhaps another way to wipe away the weekend? Whatever his reasoning, and I knew there had to be one, I placed his rock upon my dresser and added mine beside it. I wasn't sure what else to do.

Chapter Fifteen

The crackle and pop of the fire, along with the gentle roar from the ocean waves slapping against the shore, brought forth a peace in a way I'd never found back east. Being surrounded by people I now considered friends, made the first six weeks go by in a flash and made the nights less lonely. Calling Cheshire Bay home became a heartfelt statement.

The gang, as Amber affectionately called them, were all here. Lily, Eric, Cedar, Mitch, Jesse, and Mona. The only one missing was Antonio, who was set to arrive for a visit later in the month. Even the babies were present. Although, with the sun having set, they were snuggled into the playpens in the house just fifty feet away sleeping peacefully if the baby monitor resting on the cooler at Cedar's feet was any indication.

I grabbed my steaming mug of tea, a local concoction of dehydrated apples and vanilla, and scanned my circle of friends, all laughing and having a good time. Those who chose to drink were nursing their beers while one of the ladies joined me in solidarity with drinking something non-alcoholic. However, I knew the real reason – she was nurturing the life growing inside her body and hadn't yet announced the news.

Having made the conscious choice to remove alcohol from my life, it was a daily battle working in Amber's Ale. I was told by my new therapist, from that conflict I drew my greatest strength. I wasn't an alcoholic, as I didn't crave the drink or the feeling, I just made too many bad choices when I drank. The easiest fix was to eliminate it completely.

I pulled my legs under me and covered my lap in a heavy blanket, staving off the cool October ocean breeze.

My phone pinged with an incoming text, and I quickly pulled it free of my hoodie pocket to see who it was from. Deep down, I harboured hope one of my Toronto friends would message, but after six weeks, it hadn't happened. Not once, and it was hard to let that go. Tonight's message was not from one of them, but from Holden.

Although my heart skipped a beat at seeing his name on the display, the logical part of me knew better than to react like a hormonal teenage girl. Holden was betrothed to another by now, and I needed to force my heart get over that.

The skies are gorgeous. And if you look to the east, just above the horizon, that bright "star" you see is no star. It's Jupiter – the largest planet in our solar system. You should see it in a telescope. It's breathtaking.

Of course, I had to see this *breathtaking* sight for myself and searched the skies. There, hovering behind Lily and Eric's place, was Jupiter, its glow nearly as bright as the moon.

I texted back my thanks and tucked my phone away. Our texts had remained pretty one-sided.

Amber raised an eyebrow.

"Holden." I took a sip of my tea and stared at the red-hot coals.

"And?" Ever the eternal optimist, she always hung out a fairytale-like hope – how he'd give up his family and come running to me. It was a foolish idea that only manifested because her own relationship was the product of a dream come true. Antonio worked in Greece, most of the time, but he always managed to come to Cheshire Bay, to see his love, for a few days every month.

I tore my focus away from the heat of the fire and gazed upon the bright star, wondering if Holden was looking at it right now too.

"Did he say anything important?"

"He mentioned where Jupiter was."

"Oh." Her shoulders sagged.

"And where is it?" Mitch asked.

I pointed it out and listened to my friends take in my every word on the few astronomy facts I'd picked up in science class recently. Who knew they'd be interested in something I had to share, even if I had just learned it myself? It was a new feeling to get used to.

I pulled out my phone and sent a message to Holden, telling him I was suddenly a big hit with my friends, and they were all intrigued.

I'll point out other neat celestial bodies when I visit, came his reply, and I closed out of the app without responding. A visit was a form of torture for which I wasn't prepared.

"Guys can be so obtuse, am I right?" Lily was watching me carefully. "They don't get it when you tell them it's over. It's like they got to rub salt in the wounds."

"Hey," Eric, her husband, said as he passed her a beer.

"I wasn't talking about you, and you know it." She cupped his cheek in such an intimate way, I turned away.

The gang all knew about my adventure to the island, and of Holden's upcoming nuptials. Slowly, with each bonfire, I had shared a little more about myself, readying for them to ignore me or stop inviting me out. They never did. In fact, the invites grew to include lunches with the ladies, and a spa date once.

"Holden still wants to be friends, and I can't handle that." There, I'd said it and as I did, a wave of relief washed over me. It felt good to let it out.

"Why? Isn't it better to be friends than nothing at all?" Jesse walked by and grabbed a homemade cookie from the tray I'd set out.

"Not to me. It's just a constant reminder of what I can't have." Just thinking about it was a dull knife tearing at my heart. "It sounds selfish and doesn't make me a good friend, but I want him to be mine. An unrequited love as friends doesn't work. Not for me. I don't want to be there, listening to his woes or his joys about the woman in his life. And before you go and say something else, I am happy for him that he has that someone. I just wish I was that someone."

"Oh, Iris, I can totally understand." Mona spoke from across the flaming bonfire. "Even though I was over the moon for my friends, I stopped going to their baby showers because I couldn't handle the ache of seeing all the newborns, knowing I'd never have my own baby to grow and nurture."

Jesse, her fiancé, squeezed her knee.

She winked and refocused back on me. "It's so hard. You got to do what works to heal your heart. And if that means putting distance between you, then that's what you do."

"Thank you."

"We're all here for you." Mona sent a warm smile in my direction.

"You have no idea what that means to me." I glanced between the flickers of flames to look at my friends.

It was time to move on, and as Mona said, put some distance between Holden and me. But how? How do I say goodbye to the one person I'd felt the deepest connection with?

All I knew was this was going to be more painful than the few days I'd spent alone in the hospital.

Chapter Sixteen

After wiping off the bar for the fiftieth time today, I folded the towel into four and set it to the side. I'd easily adapted to my new role as barkeep and server, under Amber's tutelage, and if I were honest, it was probably the best job I'd had, alcohol issues aside. I got to socialize and meet the townsfolk, who were as warm and welcoming as I'd been led to believe. The ocean view off the back of the bar was to die for, and somehow, I'd effortlessly become one of the gang, hanging out on Eric and Lily's beach and playing with the baby and toddlers. It was as if my destiny had been here all along.

The only thing missing was Holden, and as the days stretched out into weeks, that dull ache never fully diminished. Every morning before I walked downstairs to the bar, I'd unwrap the rock I'd held tightly in my hands overnight, and replay that incredible weekend, wondering if there was anything I should've said and done. The more I thought about our time together, the more I missed it. It was a vicious cycle I couldn't break, but mainly because I just didn't want to.

Holden had texted a couple of times more since the Jupiter night, asking how things were, and I'd reply with a canned response of *fine.* I couldn't give him more, even if I wanted to. He wasn't mine, and he wasn't up for grabs.

"You in deep thought." Antonio broke through my haze as he waved a hand in front of my face.

I blinked to bring the packed pub back into focus, surveying the space for possible new guests. None were present.

Looking over at the handsome guy, I broke into a weak smile. "Just reminiscing."

"Good things come from memory. Maybe dream come true."

I scoffed. Maybe. For the rich, like he was. His story with Amber was a fairytale, one that not everyone was lucky to have. However, seeing them together, planning their upcoming wedding, they truly were two pieces of a puzzle matched perfectly, and I couldn't be happier for them.

Amber walked in from the back room, passing out papers to myself and a couple of coworkers. "Next month's schedule."

I stared at December's postings. Amber had been generous with the shifts, but not over the top. Even though I had free room and board, I was still expected to pay my way for food and expenses, and she gave me more than enough hours to do that plus re-build my savings. Truly, I was beyond grateful.

Tucking the schedule into the back pocket of my jeans, I gazed across the pub again, ensuring all was well with the dozen or so customers.

From the back of the pub, in the corner, the jukebox started playing an all-too-familiar guitar rift; the song Holden said could've been written with me in mind.

Heartbeat pounding, once again I scanned the room, narrowing my eyes at the customers lingering near the machine. Who pressed it into play? It was a song that cut to the heart, and it needed to be removed from the play list. I didn't care how popular it was in the late nineties.

Suddenly, someone twisted out of his chair and rose, and my jaw hit the floor. How had he snuck in? When?

As a stranger in these parts, the customers all turned to take in the tall, handsome man striding across the pub in my direction.

I quickly glanced behind me to Amber, my breath frozen in my chest.

Both her and Antonio were leaning against the bar, watching the scene unfold, curiosity stretching across their faces.

I gave him my full attention and took him in from head

to toe as my heart fluttered in excitement. "Holden."

"Iris."

"What are you doing here?" The lump in the back of my throat grew, nearly choking me as the words struggled to break free. It was impossible to remain aloof, which was my failing goal.

"I came here to find you."

I didn't know how to answer with anything *but* a smart assed reply. "Well, here I am."

His hands hung by his sides, shaking like a leaf in the ocean breeze. "I can't stop thinking about you."

Slowly, my head nodded, even if the same could be said about my thoughts of him. They were non-stop.

"I need you. I need to explore what happened between us, to see it grow." He stepped closer, and I breathed in his spicy, masculine smell.

"But..." Seriously, my brain needed a reboot as it failed to compose any words.

He reached out his hand and wrapped a strand of hair behind my ear, his fingers trailing down my cheek. "These past couple of months have been incredible, and I've been given everything I've worked hard for, even everything I didn't want. I'm truly beyond blessed."

My head bobbed slowly once more as I was happy for his successes.

"Only thing, with all of that, something's missing." He

covered his chest with his hands.

A tingling thrummed in the pulse of my heartbeat.

"The one thing that's missing..." Those dark green eyes of his stared into the depths of my hardened soul. "Is you."

I broke eye contact and looked around as I swallowed my gasp.

All the customers were staring at us as the song played loudly in the background. No one moved or whispered, and I hated the feeling of being in the spotlight.

"But..." Really, I needed to have a better word to stutter. "But..."

"My grandparents?" He vocalized the question for me and took a half step back. "Despite a civil conversation of breaking customs and living in the twenty-first century, they cut me off. But whatever, I can manage it. The university pays well enough that I've moved out on my own and have altered my career path just a touch as I now head up their Planetary Sciences Department based in Spirit Bay."

Spirit Bay wasn't far from here, in the ballpark of forty minutes; a helluva lot closer than Victoria.

The pounding rush of adrenaline drowned out the sensible words slowly starting to form, but my mouth was as dry as the desert, so they couldn't be given life even if I wanted to. My jaw opened slightly, and I rolled my bottom lip between my teeth with cautious hope.

"I explained things to my parents, to get their full

support and they're coming around. Slowly. They stood by my side as I did one of the toughest things ever and stood up to my grandparents." His hands formed into a steeple, and with the closest finger, he touched his lips. "I broke off the engagement, if you will, with the explanation of needing to know the person before I could marry. They misinterpreted and introduced me to Dahlia. Everyone, from my grandparents to my parents to family and friends, agreed she was a perfect match, and her family comes from a strong background. We are well suited for each other."

I crossed my arms over my chest. Here I thought he was trying to win me over, instead, he was gloating about his idyllic life and circumstances.

"However..." He inhaled sharply, his contact never breaking. "It didn't matter how perfect they thought she was for me; she lacked the spark you just feel in your soul when you meet someone. There was nothing between us, and it was easy to understand why. It was common sense." He winked. "She wasn't you. You're the one I want."

My heart skipped a beat. He wanted *me*; the tragically messed up wreck of a woman. He had walked away from his family, and likely his money, for me. "Myriam?"

"My sister will be fine. I can still provide for her, although she insists she's fine." Before I could utter another word, he continued. "You said you wanted things to be easy, and to not have it be such a battle."

Yes, those were my words, one of the last said before we parted.

"So, here I am." He tossed his hands out to the side. "I've made this easy for you, if you'll have me. Tell me you need me too."

A burst of jittery excitement made me lighter than air, and I had to check to see if I were truly floating.

"Iris, I need you to say something. Anything. Please." There was a hinting plea in his voice.

I nodded again, trying to bring forth the right words to vocalize. It was still hard to believe he was here, standing in front of me, let alone telling me how much he wanted me. I'd never been wanted by anyone. Not like this. My brain was firing in rapid motion, trying to put together a sequence of words that made any sense.

"I'm working on my GED." I hung my head. That's not what I meant to say.

A smile spread from cheek to cheek as he tipped my chin to make eye contact. "That's fantastic."

"And I'm seeing a shrink. A good one." I exposed my arms, pushing my sweater up to my elbows. The scabs had long since fallen off, replaced with ghostly healed lines; a haunting visual of all I'd put myself through, and yet a daily reminder how life was worth living.

"I'm so proud of you." His eyes reflected the overhead lights as he reached out and grabbed my hand.

Words were not only blossoming, but they also fell out as fast as my tears. "Amber is getting married in the Mediterranean, on board her yacht soon and once they set a date, I'll need one too."

He stepped closer and wrapped his arms around my waist. "Are you asking me to join you?"

I held my breath. "I am."

"Iris?"

My heart pounded so strongly, I figured he could feel it as I pressed against him. "Holden?"

"Say the words. I've come a long way to tell you about everything I gave up."

"I need you too." I threaded my fingers through his thick, dark hair and brushed my lips over his.

Without skipping a beat, he pressed his against mine, sealing the deal, and he spun me around. For a moment, I forgot where I was. However, leave it to the patrons to whoop and cheer as my feet touched the ground, and I buried my face into Holden's chest.

After catching my breath and wiping away tears of joy, I faced Amber and Antonio. "This is Holden. The guy who–" Twisting, I stared into his face. "Likes me despite who I am."

Holden's fingers linked through mine with a gentle, comforting squeeze. "I didn't want someone pretending to be who they thought I needed. You were honest with me the whole time, and you weren't afraid to be real. I wish I could've been as honest with you."

"You explained it. I didn't like it, but I understood."

"I'm all yours now."

"And I'll take you." I gazed up into his perfect face.

"As I am?"

"Yes, because you're perfect for me. I can't imagine being in anyone else's arms."

"I was hoping you'd say that."

My heart exploded, and I knew my journey with Holden was far from over.

Epilogue

Seven months later

The atmosphere in the pub was buzzing and the upcoming wedding of the local bar owner was the talk of the town. There wasn't much else to discuss, apparently.

I wiped down the counter and listened as the patrons questioned where Amber was getting married, either here in Cheshire Bay or off in the Mediterranean somewhere near Antonio's main home? Both were amazing, although it would be hard to beat a tropical wedding near a cerulean sea. But Amber hadn't disclosed the location – all she'd mentioned was it was going to be on New Year's Eve. Still, in the twenty-four hours since her announcement, the town hadn't shut up. I loved it. And I loved how they loved and adored her.

Fingers crossed she decided to at least have some kind of ceremony here, her regulars were like family.

Holden passed me his empty glass. "May I have another?"

I pulled out the dispenser and refilled. At Amber's Ale he always got brand name soda, at home, on the tight budget he was learning to live with since he'd been cut off and was still trying to help his sister, he got the budget brand, and honestly, it was comparable but not the same.

"I was wondering if we could talk?"

Even under the pub lighting, it wasn't hard to see Holden pale. He swallowed and set his glass down. "Okay."

I swatted his hand. "Oh relax, it's nothing serious."

He visibly relaxed. "Thank goodness. I'm not sure I could handle any more distressing news, between the Planetary Sciences Department drastically cutting my hours down, in addition to already struggling with a reduced use of the telescope, I just don't think I can—"

"Holden, relax. It's not bad news." I had a plan. Especially after a conversation last night with Amber. I leaned on the bar, my forearms resting on the cool surface. "I have a way of helping you with your budget. A summer proposition, if you will."

"Oh?" He took another sip of his soda. "Like a side expedition on our upcoming road trip?"

We'd been planning a weeklong escape, ending on the September long weekend, but neither of us could decide where we wanted to go, and how to go about travelling. Did we fly somewhere and rent a car back? Or drive somewhere first, and then catch a flight? There were so many options to figure out, but it would come. We still had time.

"Let's go upstairs and talk."

"Right now?" He glanced around.

I shrugged. "Why not?"

It was my scheduled break time, and the floor was fine. The other server could totally manage things for the fifteen minutes I'd be gone, plus the cook was around if anything serious should happen.

"Lead the way."

We exited the pub and wrapped around the side to the metal staircase. Ascending it, I entered the code on the keypad and waited for the beep. Antonio had installed a top-notch security system; his way of keeping Amber, and me by proxy, safe while he was away.

I closed the door after Holden was inside.

"What do you think?"

He stopped dead in his tracks and stared at me, eyes narrowing. "You didn't cut your hair, and it's not a different colour." He continued scanning. "You haven't lost any weight." He grimaced. "But I'm missing something, aren't I?"

I laughed. "Yeah, but I wasn't clear. The thoughts run faster through my head than I vocalize."

"So, what are you thinking?"

I inhaled and relaxed, something my shrink had

encouraged. It made me pause and think before I spoke.

"Do you like this place?" I waved my hands around as I spun. "It's got a great location, right on the beach. It's pretty soundproof if we seal the windows and flip on the AC. And best of all, it's all paid for."

"What? I'm missing something here."

"Amber's moving to the yacht up in Stewart Surf." The monster boat was too big to park at Wharf Point, so it had to moored further up the island. "She's staying there until the wedding, and after that, she doesn't know if they'll get their own place here or in Greece, but she's giving this apartment to me. You could move in at the end of the month."

On the stipulation, I pay all utilities and upkeep, although Antonio had given it a solid upgrade already.

"Seriously?" He wore shock like a neon sign.

"It's too fast, right?" I glanced down at the plush carpeting. "You can have my room, as I'm taking hers. We don't have to share a bedroom; I'm just giving you another option."

Her room was way bigger and had the best view. My bedroom overlooked the trees, which was nice, but hers had an expansive ocean view. And a balcony over the pub so I could always hear the music and be a part of the environment, if from a safe distance.

He stepped closer and wrapped his arms around the small of my back. "It sounds perfect."

"Which part?"

"Moving in."

"To your own room?" I didn't want to push, even if I'd been toying with the idea for a while about moving into together. Our relationship was fantastic, and I didn't want to jeopardize a thing. Some nights he'd stay at my place, and other nights, I'd stay at his.

He grinned, and then burst into a soft laugh. "To share. I had planned to ask you to move in with me when we were on our road trip, but I just hadn't been able to figure out a way of asking that didn't sound corny. I'd thought about working it into a game of twenty questions, or maybe the license plate game, but I still—"

"Holden?"

"Sorry... you were saying?"

I bridged the distance between us. "Is this okay, here? It's a longer drive for you."

"But I'm sure it's way less rent."

"Yep, practically free." Not really, but based on what he was currently paying, it would seem that way. "So, we're doing this? We're moving in together?" I held my breath and let me gaze dance between his eyes.

He nodded.

"Say the words." The expression had become our thing.

"I love you, Iris."

Not the words I was expecting, but always the best

words to hear out loud. "I love you too, Holden."

"Let's move in together. Let's embark on this new journey."

Dear Reader

Writing Iris was tough and required that I work through some personal issues – namely those dark corners people avoid having discussions about; the kind that leave you feeling helpless and all alone. But let me tell you this – you are NEVER ALONE. My inbox is always open – the toughest part is reaching out – I am here for you, like Amber was for Iris, and my friends were for me.

That being said, I'm enjoying my time in the small town so much, I have four more stories planned, and *possibly* a HUGE one to wrap up to the whole series. Some have revenge on the mind, some, like Lily, will be starting over, while others will be spreading their wings. They all will find love, but the journey to it will be different for each. And for one in particular, it will channel a very personal set of issues I had to deal with. Writing is my therapy (and just as expensive. LOL)

As an author, it makes my day when a reader or blogger shares their thoughts and gives me feedback on the characters they've invested their time in. When readers fall in love with a character, it's encouraging to write more. So, if you don't mind, share with me what you liked, what you loved, or even what you hated. I'd love to hear from you via email (hmshander@gmail.com), or a review on your favourite retailer site. It doesn't have to be long, even just as simple as "Couldn't put it down", or "Loved the characters" or "Why isn't Cheshire Bay a real place?" works. Reviews help me gain visibility, and as I'm sure you can tell from my books, reviews are tough to come by.

Thank you so much for spending time with me.
Yours,
H.M. Shander

Have you read these?

acknowledgements

I never knew when I published my very first book – *Run Away Charlotte* – that I'd be here eight years later with this backlist of books. I'm still shocked I'm fulfilling a lifelong dream and will continue to do for the foreseeable future as more characters are talking and I can barely keep up. But it couldn't have been done without the help of some truly awesome people I'm blessed to have in my life. Writing these thank yous never gets easier – NEVER – as I'm always afraid I'll miss someone, or a category will be left out. And then I wonder, does anyone even read these? I know as an author, I do, but do readers?

Writing a book for the most part, is a solo endeavor, but I could not have this ready for you to read if not for the cheerleading and support of some magnificent people in my life.

My Shander family – whom you may know on my social media platforms as Hubs, The Teen, and Little Dude – thank you sincerely for giving me the space I needed to write, to listen to my weird ideas over the dinner table (I still think the Holden daLigne job idea is gold! LOL) Thank you for inspiring me to do better, to be better, and to be someone you're proud of, just as I am so proud of you. I love you with all that I am.

To my extended family & friends – thank you for believing in me, and helping me reach my dreams. Love you, and I'm truly grateful for your unending support.

To my wonderfully dedicated alpha reader – Mandy. Girl, where would I be without you? Without your constructive feedback and endless support, you're more than just my author buddy and someone I look up to and adore – you're my trusted friend, and I'm thrilled we're in this business together. I want nothing but success for you, and I can't wait to watch you tick off all your goals as complete and successful in the upcoming year. You deserve it all.

To my fantastic critique partner – Letzia. Thank you for all your valuable feedback and insight. For highlighting what made you laugh and what made you cry, and which phrases you loved, and those you didn't understand. Your detailed thoughts on every chapter were as valuable to me as gold. Thank you so much for spending your time with the Teddy Bear. LOL.

To my critique partner- Josephine. How many times did I redo those hard chapters to stop them from putting you to sleep? LOL. Thanks to your dedicated help, the story is richer, sharper, and has a much more layered heroine.

To my beta readers – Rebecca, Kelly, and Holly. Thank you for your feedback and insight into making the characters a little more relatable and less perfect (well, Holden anyway. Iris is pretty far removed from perfect.) I'm thrilled you enjoyed the story and couldn't put it down, and I look forward to your feedback on the upcoming books.

To my editor – Irina. Every manuscript you find something I need to work on – but at least it's not always the same old mistakes – it's always new ones. LOL. Thanks for your eagle eye, for catching those inconsistencies I could've sworn I caught, and for being ready on time. I never have to fear when you hold my baby in your hands. It always comes back with red marks, but they always enhance the story. You rock. Thank you.

To Eleanor, my gifted designer. Thank you for your hard work at turning an ordinary cover into one that sparkles, and reflects the characters, the series, and the theme. You are a gift.

If I missed you, it certainly wasn't intentional. I know I couldn't be where I am without the help of so many others. Thank you! And thank you for reading and making it all the way to the end. You all rock.

about the author

USA TODAY bestselling author H.M. Shander is a stargazing, romantic at heart who once attended Space Camp and wanted to pilot the space shuttle, not just any STS – specifically Columbia. However, the only shuttle she operates in her real world is the #momtaxi; an electric car that transports her two kids to school and various sporting events. When she's not commandeering Elektra, you can find the school librarian surrounded by classes of children as she reads the best storybooks in multiple voices. After she's tucked her endearing kids into bed and kissed her trophy husband goodnight, she moonlights as a contemporary romance novelist; the writer of sassy heroines and sweet, swoon-worthy heroes who find love in the darkest of places.

For all the latest release news, subscribe to H.M. Shander's newsletter (link on website), or you can follow her on Twitter(@HM_Shander), Facebook (hmshander), or check out her website at www.hmshander.com.

Thanks for reading– all the way to the very end.

www.ingramcontent.com/pod-product-compliance
Lightning Source LLC
Chambersburg PA
CBHW020433180626
46812CB00003B/1205